Until We Kissed

Until We Kissed

A PINE VALLEY NOVEL

Heather B. Moore

Mirror Press

Interior design by Cora Johnson
Edited by Kelsey Down and Lisa Shepherd
Cover design by Rachael Anderson
Cover image credit: Shutterstock #52495263, Evgeny Karandaev
Published by Mirror Press, LLC
ISBN-13: 978-1-947152-53-3

PINE VALLEY SERIES

Worth the Risk
Where I Belong
Say You Love Me
Waiting for You
Finding Us
Until We Kissed
Let's Begin Again

Until We Kissed

Pine Valley librarian Livvy Harmon has big dreams, which include marrying Dr. Slade McKinney. Trouble is, he's only kissed her once in their four months of dating, and it wasn't all that great. But Livvy isn't ready to give up yet on hooking such an amazing man, even though Slade seems to have time for everyone but her.

When Livvy keeps running into writer Mason Rowe, who seems to be camping out in her library to finish his book under strict orders from his agent, Livvy at first keeps him at arm's length. But the more their friendship grows, the more she finds that her dream relationship with her doctor boyfriend isn't so dreamy after all.

One

"Hello?" Livvy tried not to sound over-the-top excited even though she'd been waiting three days for Slade to call and confirm their date. Or *Dr. McKinney,* as he was known to his patients. Thankfully the Pine Valley library was empty since it was five minutes to closing time, and Livvy didn't have to put him on hold for an annoying patron needing to check out a book at the last minute.

"Liv?" Slade said into the phone, his voice rich, deep.

The way Slade shortened her name made goose bumps stand on Livvy's arms. It was like he had his own personal nickname for her. Okay, so *Liv* wasn't really all that unique. Her mom called her Liv; so did her brother and her roommate . . . But that was beside the point.

She leaned against the reference counter, where she'd been putting in the recent book order on the computer. "Hi, Slade," she said in that light, breezy tone she'd perfected just for Dr. Slade McKinney, aka *Mr. Dreamy Doc.* She didn't want to creep out Slade and let him discover that long before they had gone on their first date she'd been stalking him. Well, *stalking* was too strong of a word. Maybe *light* stalking, or being extremely observant.

But who could really blame her? It had been her girlhood dream to marry a doctor. Even Ken from her Barbie-playing days had been a doctor. And it was only natural that Livvy had dated a pre-med student in college. And when that relationship didn't work out, she had dated another one. She had eventually graduated in library science, unmarried, but she didn't let that deter her from her goal of marrying a doctor.

Only her best friend, Felicity, knew about Livvy's goal. Some things were better kept to one's self, because she didn't really have an answer to the why of it. She could possibly, potentially, blame it on her days of sitting on the upstairs landing, peeking through the banister, and watching the television show *ER,* which her mother had forbidden her to watch. Thursday nights her mother made doubly sure that Livvy went to bed early.

Livvy had gone to bed quite happily, knowing that in twenty minutes she could sneak out onto the landing and watch anyway—albeit a slightly skewed and muffled version of *ER.*

And one of the families on their block had a doctor for a father and a mother who dressed beautifully and was always heading up local charity events.

Then there was the rash of medical thrillers that Livvy had gotten hooked on a few years back. Authors like Joe Monsun, Collette Burrows, and Mason Rowe all topped her must-read list. As the librarian for Pine Valley Library, Livvy made sure the new releases were on her annual budget list.

"So, uh, Liv," Slade said in that low, melodic tone of his. "I've got to reschedule tonight after all."

The stab of disappointment was sharp in Livvy's gut, and she closed her eyes and exhaled to gain her equilibrium back. *It's okay. It's fine. This is what it is like dating a doctor.*

Slade was still talking. Saying something about having to switch with the on-call doctor at the hospital because the other doctor had to go out of town for his anniversary . . .

Livvy tried not to pout, but inside she was definitely pouting. She didn't want to be a high-maintenance girlfriend, but she and Slade had been dating for five months and three days, and still . . . they only went out every couple of weeks. Texts had replaced phone calls in the interim, and texts were way less exciting than phone calls from Slade.

"Okay, no problem," Livvy said, an unwanted squeak in her voice. She was *not* going to cry. "Maybe we can change our reservations for tomorrow night."

"Uh, tomorrow I'm on my regular on-call shift," he said. "Sorry, sweetheart."

The *sweetheart* endearment meant she forgave him everything and anything in an instant.

"I understand." Her voice sounded faint to her ears. Had he noticed? She had to be more upbeat, more confident, more like the kind of woman a successful doctor would propose to because she was his better half. She kept the home fort down, raising their children while he was saving lives.

"Do you still want to go hiking Sunday morning?" he asked.

Livvy found herself hesitating. *Unbelievable—I've never hesitated before.* So what if he hiked like a possessed mountain goat and she had to live on Advil the next three days after an excursion with him? He never missed his monthly hikes, and if she were to fit into his busy schedule then she had to take opportunities where she could. Besides, on their last date, two weeks before, he'd kissed her goodnight. A toe-curling, face-fanning kiss. Their relationship was definitely moving forward.

Okay, so the kiss had been a little too brief for her liking, and his hands had been strangely clammy, but she'd decided to ignore that. Because, *hello,* doctor.

But would he kiss her when she was panting like a hyena and her nose was frozen pink on the top of the Pine Valley ski resort?

"Sure, what time?" she asked.

"Same time as always," he said. "Pick you up at 5:30?"

"Yep," Livvy said. "I'll be ready."

"Great," Slade said. "Dress warm. It might snow."

He said something else about how he couldn't believe it was November already, but Livvy heard nothing after *snow.* Yes, she might live in Pine Valley, a known ski-resort town, but she hated the cold. Snow. Wind. Ice. All of it.

Somehow she ended the conversation in a perfectly cheerful tone. When Slade hung up, Livvy stared at her phone for a moment. What had she agreed to? She'd swapped out a perfectly nice evening of a cozy dinner at an Italian restaurant for a freezing-cold trek up a snowy mountain.

She slipped her phone into her pocket, then leaned forward and let her head drop onto the reference counter. Gripping the ends of her hair, she let out a groan as she imagined how the cold would penetrate her very bones. Her feet would be like blocks of ice, and her hands would be numb for a week. Her nose and chin and lips would be colder than popsicles.

"Are you okay?" a male voice asked.

Livvy jumped away from the desk and gasped. When she saw a man, who was staring at her like she'd lost her mind, she backed away. He looked like one of those men straight from a lumberjack contest that she used to watch on TV with her little brother. The guy wore a thick red-and-navy plaid shirt and ripped jeans, complete with heavy boots. His dark hair reached his collar, and he had a beard that actually looked quite good on him—if she were into beards on men—which she wasn't.

If the man's eyes had been dark and eerie she might have called 911. But they were a surprising light blue, and his mouth had curved upward as if he were about to laugh at her. Still, she pulled her phone out of her pocket just in case.

"You shouldn't creep up on me like that," she said.

"It's impossible to creep with these boots on," he said, lifting a foot as if to demonstrate. She looked down again at his boots, then back up. *Oh boy.* He was tall. And sort of hunky. The broad-shoulder-slim-waist type. Which only proved her lumberjack theory.

"Besides, you looked a little . . . distressed." He narrowed those blue eyes of his. "Are you sure you're okay?"

"Of course I'm okay," she said. "I received some bad news, that's all."

He continued to stare at her, and she wondered why he was in the library in the first place. Looking for a book on trees? Wow. That would be ironic. It was then she noticed he had a legal pad and pen in his hand. Had he been taking notes from an encyclopedia?

"Okay, not *bad* news, exactly, but disappointing." She waved a hand. "On second thought, it was really nothing. I just overreacted."

His mouth quirked again.

She placed a hand on her hip, wondering why she felt like she had to explain anything to a stranger. "You startled me, all right? I'm not usually a jumpy person, but the library *is* closed. I thought I was alone."

"I was on my way out," he said, taking a step back. But he didn't turn around, and he didn't look away. It was like he wanted to ask her something yet didn't know how.

Oh . . . "We don't have a homeless shelter in Pine Valley, but the cops will help out if you need something. I can make a phone call for you."

He didn't say anything for a moment, then he chuckled. "You think I'm homeless?"

Livvy's face heated. "I—I guess not?"

He scratched at his beard. "I knew I let myself go, but I didn't think I looked homeless."

Well, now that she had a closer look at him, she realized she might have rushed to assumptions. He didn't smell, and the ripped jeans could be more of a fashion statement. He wasn't hauling around a giant backpack full of his life essentials, and even though he was of a lean build, he didn't have that gaunt look.

"It's been a long day," she said, then cleared her throat. "But the library is closed, sir. I need to ask you to leave."

He nodded. "Sorry I scared you." Then he turned around and strode to the front doors.

Livvy stared after lumberjack guy until he'd disappeared through the entrance. It was dark outside, so she couldn't see how far he went into the parking lot. She remained at the reference counter, and moments later she saw headlights move through the parking lot and a dark-colored Jeep drive out.

So . . . not homeless then. She crossed to the front doors, locked them, then turned out the main lights. The night lights would stay on, and since she was curious about what the man had been doing, she walked to the study area to see if anything was out of place. A chair was slightly askew—perhaps he'd been sitting there. But no reference books were on any of the tables, and it didn't look like anything had been touched since she'd last made her rounds.

Lumberjack man must have come into the library when she was busy helping the group of seventh graders who'd been assigned to do a group project. Otherwise, she couldn't imagine how she'd missed noticing a man of that stature in her library.

Her phone buzzed with a text. It was from her best friend and nearly next-door neighbor, Felicity Miner. *Have fun on your date with Slade tonight.*

The reminder made Livvy's heart sink again. She texted back that Slade had cancelled on her again, and did Felicity have a winter coat she could borrow?

Don't tell me you're going hiking, Felicity texted.

I am. I'm weak.

Haha. You must really be in love.

Livvy laughed, then she paused. *Was* she in love with Slade McKinney? The short answer was yes. The long answer was not something she really wanted to analyze right now. She was still feeling put out by the cancelled dinner date. She supposed that in her Barbie and Ken playacting, she hadn't really thought that being a doctor's girlfriend would be so . . . lonely.

A woman never gives away all her secrets, she wrote to Felicity. *Please tell me you have ice cream in your freezer and no plans tonight.*

I'm 100% free and YES on the ice cream.

Great, I'll be there in twenty minutes.

Two

Mason tossed his keys onto the kitchen counter of his rented cabin. Today had been a surprisingly good day. Good because he'd written an entire chapter—and although he had no idea where it was going to fit into his work in progress, it was still more than he'd written in a single day for over a year.

And he'd laughed. Another unusual event of late.

The librarian had somehow brought it out of him by calling him homeless.

Maybe technically he was homeless. The rented cabin in Pine Valley was definitely not his home, but his agent had insisted he unplug and get away from all social media until his next book was drafted.

Mason opened the fridge, which he should keep better stocked. He wished he'd done a grocery run on his way back from the library. He shut the fridge and grabbed an apple from the welcome basket on the counter, courtesy of his agent.

Biting into the apple, he walked out of the kitchen and through the dark rooms until he reached the sliding door. The moon cast its silvery light across the wood deck, outdoor furniture, and hot tub.

This cabin would be an excellent place for a writers' retreat.

He tried to remember the last time he'd been around his peers. It was October of last year, at a gala where he'd received another Best Thriller Writer of the Year award. Two days before Teddy Stern had filed his lawsuit.

The lawsuit was ridiculous, and everyone knew it. Mason hadn't stolen anyone's book idea, let alone an indie author who had written a handful of short stories and published them without editing the manuscripts.

In fact, the lawsuit was shot down within a couple of months, but the social media firestorm had been vicious, both for and against Mason. When his next book, *Cut,* released in February, his usual release month for all his books, he had reached the *New York Times* list as expected, but his release week numbers had dropped by twenty percent.

Coincidence? Mason knew it wasn't.

Reviews on *Cut* were harsh—and although there were plenty of good ones, it seemed that the percentage of bad reviews had escalated.

Mason had tried not to let it bother him. His book could still be viewed as a success, but he found that, day after day, he wasn't doing any writing.

And he had missed his April submission deadline for the first time in his fourteen-year writing career. Last month when he didn't have a book on the advance review lists and upcoming releases lists, social media had pounced again.

Rumors swirled that he'd quit writing, that he was truly

guilty of plagiarizing Teddy, that he'd moved to Canada or Mexico . . .

He'd ignored it all, of course, but he still wasn't writing.

Every time he sat down he might type a handful of sentences, but they had no life, no direction, and no purpose. So he deleted those sentences and turned on whatever ball game happened to be on one of his dozens of cable channels.

Mason did have to give his agent credit for her patience. If he lost money, she did too. Yes, he'd had a good run, had made great money, but he was thirty-seven and should still have plenty of productive years left. Besides, what bothered him most wasn't the money or the lawsuit or anything that anyone said on social media—it was the loss of his words.

He'd even gone to a psychologist, who pretty much told him to play relaxing music while he wrote.

His agent, Jolene, had a more life-altering suggestion.

Jolene told him she couldn't hold him a release spot if he didn't get his next manuscript in by January 1. He'd already missed one release year, but his agent thought if his next book came out only six months behind schedule he wouldn't lose much traction. Jolene had found the Pine Valley cabin for rent and said she'd even have food delivered if it would help.

Mason had told her he'd take care of his own food, but when he'd arrived, there was a large gift basket of food on the counter. He wasn't surprised.

He opened the sliding door and stepped out onto the patio. November was cold in Pine Valley, but he didn't mind it. The sharp coolness seemed to be working by clearing his senses. And he found the only thing he really missed about his San Diego home was walking along the beach in the early mornings. But even the steady thrum of the incoming waves hadn't been able to shake him out of his writer's block.

So here he was in a mountain resort, looking at towering

pine trees. The weather app on his phone had predicted snow this weekend—which he was sort of looking forward to. Growing up in Colorado, he'd loved the snow as a kid. But after moving to San Diego on a college basketball scholarship, he had never left. When he blew out his ACL his junior year in college, he'd spent hours in physical therapy, and he became quite fascinated by the medical industry. That, and he had a lot of time to read.

Which led to the bizarre idea that he should write his own book about an injured basketball player who became caught up in an illegal money-laundering scheme with an attractive thirty-something pharmacist. He had no idea what to do with the 350-page book he'd written, so he did some googling. A week later he had signed with an agent, and after months of quite painful revisions and him questioning what Jolene saw in the story in the first place, the book sold to a major publisher. A year later the book was released to decent reviews. His second book sold more. His third book sat on the *New York Times* list for fifteen weeks, where it was soon joined by the paperback versions of books one and two.

Mason pulled out his phone—the one on which he'd deleted all social media apps, as promised to his agent. She deserved a phone call tonight even though it was after 10:00 p.m. in New York. Mason knew that Jolene slept less than he did.

"Mason?" Jolene answered on the second ring. "Is this good news or bad news? Please tell me you've written at least fifty pages."

No matter what Mason called to talk to his agent about, it felt that she always did more talking than he did. And she very well knew that not even a robot could have written fifty pages between now and when they'd last talked the day before. "Twelve pages."

Jolene gasped.

Mason wasn't sure if it was a good gasp or a bad gasp.

Then she said, "That's wonderful. Too early to tell me the plot?"

"Much too early." They both knew he was a pantser. The plot would develop in the first hundred pages, with a lot of rewriting, then be established by the next two hundred pages. Sort of a backwards way to outline, he guessed.

"Well," Jolene said. "I'm pleased . . . was there anything you did differently today?"

"I went to the library." He could almost see Jolene's dark brows raise.

"Huh. I didn't know there was a library in Pine Valley."

"There is." *And a sassy librarian.* "I showed up around five with my legal pad, and . . . started to write."

"Hmm. By *hand?*"

"Yep. I didn't bring my laptop because I wasn't planning on a breakthrough."

Jolene went silent for a few moments, then she said, "Mason, can you go to the library tomorrow?"

Mason chuckled. "I have no doubt that you are now googling the library hours for Pine Valley."

"Nine to seven," Jolene said, laughter in her voice. "Oh, wow. The website is very sophisticated."

"Pine Valley is a resort town, not a backwoods trailer park."

"Yeah, but there's a bio of the librarian listed here," she said. "The director, Olivia Harmon, has a master's in library science."

Olivia Harmon. That must be *her.* He thought of the woman's ~~dark~~ curls, which she'd pulled back into a clip, and how her ~~dark brown~~ eyes had seemed to burrow right through him. Her blue V-neck sweater and black slacks had been unassuming but had caught his attention nonetheless. Or maybe it was the five rings she wore—none of which were on her ring finger. Or the jangling of her bracelets. He'd assumed that a librarian would wear quieter jewelry.

"She's pretty," Jolene said in a slow voice.

There was a picture of Olivia Harmon on the website? Mason put Jolene on speaker and pulled up the library website on his phone. He clicked on the Contact Menu, and yep. There she was. ~~Dark~~, curly hair, small silver hoop earrings, ~~brown~~ eyes. She had a freckle on the right side of her mouth. He hadn't noticed that earlier. Even in the picture, she seemed to be smirking at something or ready to tell everyone that the library was closed.

"Mason?" Jolene's voice cut through his thoughts. "You've met Olivia Harmon, haven't you?"

"Briefly."

"And . . . is she perhaps the reason behind this sudden twelve pages?"

"No," Mason could confidently say. "I met her as I was leaving the library tonight—after the twelve pages."

The relief was evident in Jolene's voice when she said, "All right. Just know that this manuscript is your *priority*, you understand. I don't want to pull the mother card here."

"I don't think even my own mother, were she still alive, would tell me that I couldn't talk to a pretty librarian."

Jolene groaned. "I don't know how many more favors I can call in. Your publisher isn't exactly happy that your first print run of *Cut* still hasn't sold out."

Mason took her off speaker and put the phone to his ear. "I know, Jolene. Tonight was only about calling you with good news. I know the rest."

"You're right," Jolene said in a brighter tone. "Congratulations, Mason. And let me know if you need anything at all. I'm here for you."

"Thank you," Mason said. The phrase might sound cliché for some, but he knew Jolene really would answer his call day or night. She'd even offered to come out to Pine Valley and brainstorm ideas.

Mason had quickly shot down that offer. He didn't work that way. As a pantser, he could barely shuffle through his own ideas. Someone else's brain power in the mix would derail his. After he hung up with Jolene he crossed the deck to one of the outdoor chairs. He sat on the cold wrought-iron and opened the browser on his phone. The bio about Olivia Harmon was only two paragraphs, but Mason read every word of it twice.

Not that he was being a creep or anything, and not that he'd ever ask a woman out in a small resort town when he was on a deadline upon which the rest of his career as a writer depended. Jolene was right. Today had been a good day, but he needed to keep his focus.

Besides, dating and being a full-time writer didn't go hand in hand. When people knew he was a full-time writer, they imagined that he typed out his first one thousand words in the morning with a cup of coffee. Then the next two thousand were written while he lounged by a pool. Then that was followed by some late-afternoon writing at his dining table, after which he went to evening book signings, followed by drinking wine and smoking cigars with a couple of rabid fans at a nearby bar.

No. Being a full-time writer consisted of staring at walls, pacing floors, staring at the laptop screen, answering emails, avoiding phone calls, ignoring texts, then finally typing a sentence. Or maybe two.

Then the cycle would start all over again.

Eight-hour days were more like sixteen-hour days, and still at the end of each day Mason felt like he'd barely accomplished anything.

Maybe he should have been a librarian.

Three

$\mathcal{L}$ ivvy bit back a curse when her alarm went off Sunday morning at 5:00 a.m. It was pitch-dark outside, and when she'd gotten up in the middle of the night it had indeed been snowing. She pushed herself into a sitting position because she was in danger of falling back asleep.

Livvy regretted the loss of warmth about her shoulders immediately. She wanted to burrow back into her covers, but Slade would be here in thirty minutes. And if she cancelled on him, who knew when they'd next get together.

She closed her eyes, thinking of Slade. His easy laugh, his charming smile, his straight teeth, his green eyes, his doctorate degree.

Okay . . . She was getting out of bed.

Livvy threw off the covers in one motion, then swung her feet over the bed, where she'd strategically placed her slippers. She stepped into them, then grabbed her cozy robe from the end of the bed.

Her roommate, Mallory, had come home late last night—the girl was a serial-dater—so Livvy doubted Mallory would hear a thing as she got ready. But then Livvy paused. She didn't want to shower before the hike, because surely she'd want to take a two-hour bath after just to thaw out.

Livvy dressed in layers, then pulled on her warmest boots, wishing she had some of those Uggs. Her double layer of socks would have to do. She put on a sweater and a coat, then pulled her hair back into a low ponytail so that she could fit a beanie on her head. She'd wait to put on the hat later so that she didn't look too much like a wimp when Slade picked her up. He never seemed to get cold.

She made her way through the darkness of the house that she rented with Mallory and peered out the front window. The snow had tapered off, but there were at least two to three inches built up. Slade's Land Rover pulled up then. He was ten minutes early, but Livvy didn't wait for him to text or call; she opened the front door, then waved at him. She locked the door and walked carefully along the walkway, through the snow. If she was home before Mallory woke up, Livvy would shovel, but she didn't have time for it now.

Slade got out of the car, and Livvy smiled. He looked like he'd stepped out of an L.L.Bean catalog, with his beanie matching his down coat. The ends of his light-brown hair showed at the edges of his beanie, and his green eyes were lively. He wore heavy boots that probably outweighed Livvy's by twenty pounds.

"Hi, Liv," Slade said, opening the passenger door for her.

Such a gentleman, although she was half hoping he'd kiss her. A quick peck would do. Or even on the cheek? Nothing.

"Good morning," she said brightly. She slid into the leather seat. He'd turned on the seat warmers, so it was nice and toasty.

Without further ado, Slade shut her door and walked around to his side. It was okay that he hadn't kissed her as a greeting. They weren't at that point in their relationship yet. Although she was often confused about where they were in their relationship, she wasn't about to have *the talk*. Besides, it was the twenty-first century, and she could be the one instigating the kissing. She sort of saw Slade kissing *her* as a sign of his interest in her.

Now she was being ridiculous. They'd been dating for months. And he kept asking her out. Slade climbed into the car and grinned at her. "Ready? It's going to be so cool hiking through the first snowfall of the season."

So . . . cool . . . pun intended? "Can't wait," Livvy said. Maybe he'd kiss her at the top of the ski resort while snowflakes twirled around them, and Slade would tell her that they needed to see each other more often and they should probably meet each other's parents. He'd invite her for Thanksgiving with his family, and she'd charm them all by telling them of her work at the library. She'd be viewed as the sweetest small-town woman, who would make a perfect doctor's wife.

"Liv? We're here."

She blinked and looked over at Slade. But he'd already opened his door and was grabbing stuff from the back. From the looks of it, he'd brought a CamelBak and some ski poles.

She opened her door and slid out. "Ski poles?"

He smiled, his green eyes crinkling at the corners. "Just to give us more speed going up and more traction coming down in case it doesn't stop snowing."

Speaking of snow—there was way more than three inches of snow in the Alpine Lodge parking lot, where Slade had stopped. She slid on her beanie, pulled on her gloves, then accepted the ski poles from Slade.

The sun hadn't even come up, and Slade was all smiles. It wasn't that Livvy hated early mornings. In theory, she wasn't opposed to getting up extra early for something fun, but snow at 5:30 a.m. was a bit much. Even when it was accompanied by Mr. Dreamy Doc.

They set off, Livvy keeping up across the parking lot, past the lodge, and up the first slope. It was invigorating, really, and Livvy was barely breaking a sweat. In fact, she was plenty warm from the waist up. Her legs were cold, but not freezing, and her feet only sort of achy.

She ignored all that and focused on the gorgeous pines and the dusting of snow upon them, making everything look like a winter wonderland. They passed a row of cabins. Likely they had heaters and fireplaces, thick fleece blankets, and mugs just waiting for hot chocolate.

Livvy tore her gaze from the cozy cabins to focus on the slope they were climbing. "Wow, it's really gorgeous," she said as the first episode of breathlessness hit. She gulped in the cold air.

"Yeah, amazing, isn't it?" Slade said. He went quiet again.

On the last hike, Livvy had learned that Slade didn't like to talk much on the hikes. It was more of a Zen time for him, and she totally got that. But it was *so* quiet out here, and that was something remarkable to be noticed by a librarian.

They passed by another cabin, and a thin line of smoke was coming out of the chimney. Livvy couldn't help the flash of envy she felt. Someone had a fire in their fireplace and was probably sipping cocoa or coffee and looking out their giant window, watching the snow float down. Their toes and feet and legs were warm.

Appreciate nature, Livvy, she thought to herself. *It's not that cold.* She was shivering. And she couldn't feel her feet. Did she still have a nose?

Then she nearly fell to the ground. "Ow! Ow! Ow!" she squealed. Pain gripped her left calf.

Slade whipped around. "What's wrong?"

"My . . . leg," she gasped. "A charley horse." She couldn't walk, couldn't move.

"Flex your foot," Slade said, hurrying back to her because he'd gotten about ten paces in front of her when she'd started to lag.

Slade grabbed her arm so that she could balance on her good leg.

"But won't that hurt?" she said in a pitiful tone.

"Not as much as the charley horse."

So Livvy held onto Slade as she flexed her left foot. The stretch made the ache ease, although it hurt to flex.

"Better?" Slade asked, looking down, his green eyes focused on her.

She sighed. "Better." Then she put weight on her foot, and the pain returned, not so strong but deep. She winced.

"We can go back," Slade said. "Your body temperature probably dropped too fast."

Well, she hadn't expected him to offer to cut the hike short, but the man was a doctor. Saving lives, healing sick people, and all that. "I don't want you to miss your hike," she said. "Maybe I can hang out at the lodge."

A line formed between his brows. "Well, I was going to take you home, then come back up. I can still get my hike in, just delay it a little. But if you want to sit in the lodge instead, then it will save me time."

Time. Everything in their relationship was about time. *His* time. Never hers.

"I'll sit at the lodge," she said, too irritated to say what she wanted to say. Besides, her calf was still sore.

"If you're sure?" Slade said.

Livvy didn't miss the hope in his eyes. She forced a smile even though it probably looked half-frozen.

Slade didn't seem to mind her frozen smile. "Great. I'll be about an hour and a half."

"Okay, see you then." Livvy hoped her voice sounded strong and confident. She stood for a moment, watching him hike away from her. He paused several paces later and turned and waved, sheer gratitude in his expression.

Livvy smiled her frozen smile and waved back.

Then she moved her cold, numb feet toward the row of cabins that were on the way to the lodge. The sun was beginning to rise, and soon it would warm her, right? The snow turned gold white, and Livvy squinted against the glare. When she arrived at the cabin they'd passed earlier, the smoke was still rising from the chimney. If she cut around the back of it, there was a straighter shot to the lodge. So she trudged through the new snow and arrived at the property line of the cabin, which was surrounded by a low river-rock wall.

Sitting on the wall, she decided to rest for a few moments, at least until the pain in her calf subsided. She should probably flex her foot again, so gingerly she started to flex. Another cramp seized her calf. "Ow! Ow!"

She closed her eyes, gritting her teeth together, letting the pain pass.

"Are you okay, ma'am?" a man said behind her.

Livvy screeched and nearly fell off the wall.

A strong hand grasped her arm, preventing her from falling into the snow. "Easy. I didn't mean to startle you."

That voice.

Livvy turned to look at the man. The *lumberjack* man. "You."

He wore a dark-gray turtleneck that somehow made his eyes bluer. Same beard, same quirk of mouth like he was laughing at her, same broad shoulders, same boots . . . The jeans were darker, no holes this time.

"Me." He was definitely holding back a laugh. "I can't believe you're sitting on my wall. It's freezing out here."

That phrase made Livvy shiver. "You're telling me."

He lifted his dark brows. "Do you live around here?"

"Not exactly," she said. "I was on my way to the lodge when I got a charley horse." Number two.

Lumberjack man sucked in a breath. "Ouch. I'm surprised you weren't cursing up a storm."

"I don't curse."

He chuckled. "You're kidding."

She shook her head.

"Okay. I guess I can see that about you," he said.

"What do you mean by that?"

Her question seemed to catch him off guard, because his expression sobered. Then he tilted his head, studying her. If he kept looking at her like that, her face was going to thaw out.

"You're too sweet," he said. "Like, June Cleaver sweet."

Livvy narrowed her eyes, and the man only quirked his brows again as if challenging her. She didn't know if this was a compliment or insult, but it was way too weird to be seeing lumberjack man twice in the same weekend . . . She didn't even know his name. Livvy moved off the wall, gingerly putting weight on her left foot. Yep, her calf felt like it had a deep bruise, but she could walk as far as the lodge, then figure out how to thaw out her body.

She took the first step, testing, and sucked in her breath.

"Do you want a rice bag?" lumberjack man asked.

"A rice bag?"

"You know, a heated rice bag to ease the pain in your leg," he said. "You could come inside my cabin too and warm up a little."

She shot him a look that didn't need to explain how she felt about that offer. Didn't he have something better to do than watch her hobble around his cabin? He obviously wasn't homeless—not in the least, by the looks of the gorgeous cabin.

Lumberjack man lifted his hands. "Or . . . I could heat the rice bag and bring it to you."

"But wouldn't it cool off too fast?" she said, and before he could answer she added, "I can make it to the lodge okay. Besides, Slade said that I need to keep flexing my foot. Work it out."

"Slade?" he asked. "Is that your husband?"

The innocent yet knowing tone of his voice gave him away, and something fluttered in her stomach at the realization that maybe he'd noticed she didn't wear a wedding ring. Right now, she was wearing gloves, so he had to have noticed at the library. "Slade's my boyfriend."

"And where is he now?"

Livvy didn't like all these persistent questions. "He's hiking. I was with him until my leg cramped."

"He left you?" Lumberjack man looked up the slope, and Livvy sort of liked that he was incredulous about it.

She felt that way too but hadn't admitted it to herself. "The lodge is just over there."

He looked from the slope to the lodge, then back to her. "It's not 'just over there.' It's probably a half mile."

"Not so far."

He scoffed. "What time did you start hiking?"

"Five-thirty or so." She swallowed.

"Before the sun came up? No wonder you're freezing and cramping up."

His voice was hard, and she wasn't sure why he cared so much.

"Like I said, you can warm up at my place, or I'll walk you to the lodge."

"Uh, I'm sure you're a perfectly nice guy." Her sarcasm didn't fool him. "But I prefer the lodge."

He nodded, as if he wasn't surprised at her answer. "Hang on, I'll be right back."

And before Livvy could respond, he strode off, his boots cutting through the snow. She probably shouldn't be staring at him walking away, so she looked toward the slope. Maybe she should start walking; she didn't know lumberjack man, except that he was kind of nosy and opinionated and well . . . bossy.

She was about to make the trek to the lodge on her own when he reemerged from the cabin. He'd pulled on a coat, and he carried a small, pillow-like thing.

As he approached, Livvy found that his direct gaze was disconcerting, as if he could see more into what she was telling him.

"I brought the rice bag," he said, holding it up. "We'll heat it in the lodge, since you don't want to come into my perfectly warm cabin."

She shoved her hands into her coat pockets. "Thanks, but why are you doing all this? I don't even know your name."

"Mason," he said easily. "And you're Olivia Harmon, right? Library director."

Four

Olivia Harmon looked even more wary now. Her ~~brown~~ eyes narrowed, and she bit the bottom of her lip. Which only brought Mason's attention to the freckle above her mouth—the freckle he'd noticed in the picture on the library website.

"I looked up the library hours," Mason told her, hoping his explanation sounded completely innocent. "And your picture and bio were on the website." It was mostly true, just not really in that order.

She seemed both surprised and possibly irked. Then she shivered. She was going to catch hypothermia. What was her boyfriend thinking? He should have made sure she got to the lodge okay.

Mason stepped over the wall. "Come on, Olivia. I'll walk you to the lodge, then I'll show you how to get rid of that cramp."

"You really don't have to," she said. "And I go by Livvy."

27

"I'm at least walking you to the lodge, Livvy."

She shrugged and grabbed the ski poles next to her. Then she started walking. He walked alongside her, and when she didn't protest further, he took it as a good sign. She wore a beanie and gloves, but her coat wasn't down, and her boots looked more like they were a fashion statement rather than built for snow. No wonder she was cold and her leg had cramped.

After a few moments of walking in silence, she cut him a glance. "I guess you aren't exactly homeless if you live in that cabin."

"I'm renting it," he said. "So technically, I could be considered homeless."

Her gaze moved to his again, interest in those brown eyes of hers. "Where are you from?"

"Colorado originally, but I live in San Diego now."

She nodded. "So the snow isn't too shocking to you."

"No, not shocking," he said. "Although I liked it a lot more as a kid than I do now. I'm not much of a skier, and it doesn't look like you are either. You're not dressed for the weather."

"I haven't quite built up my winter wardrobe."

"You're not one of the Pine Valley ski bums?"

"Hardly." She laughed.

He liked her laugh. It meant she felt more comfortable around him, more relaxed.

"Last winter I spent indoors," she continued. "I prefer warm fires, hot drinks, and a good book. I mean, don't get me wrong. This snow is really pretty, as a *view* through a window."

Mason smirked. "The right boots and a pair of wool socks can make all the difference."

"Wool, huh?" Livvy mused. "Maybe I'll try that for the next mountain hike."

"You're a glutton for punishment."

She laughed again. And . . . they'd reached the lodge. So Mason walked her in and said, "Sit by the fireplace. I'll be back in a minute."

For a second, he thought she was going to argue with him, but instead she crossed to the huge hearth and sat in a leather chair in front of the blazing fire. Mason approached the concierge desk and asked the man to microwave the rice bag for four minutes. Mason expected the strange look he was given, but like any good concierge, the man didn't ask questions.

Mason waited by the concierge counter, looking about the lodge. The giant hewn timbers, flagstone floor, and thick rugs made this place look like it could be in one of the decorator magazines. And it probably had been. His rented cabin was quite posh, and his was one of the smaller ones in the area. It seemed the wealthy had found refuge in Pine Valley.

Mason could technically consider himself among the wealthy—his royalty advances were six figures—but he wasn't a pretentious person himself. Besides, he'd rather hang around the ordinary folk. Made it easier to develop characters for his books.

Speaking of observing people . . . Livvy seemed to be relaxed in her chair and had pulled out her phone. She'd taken off her beanie, and her dark curls were kind of a wild mess about her face. Then she winced and bent down and rubbed her calf.

"Here you are, sir." The concierge had returned.

Mason thanked the man, then took the heated rice bag. It was too hot to hold in one hand for long, so he kept switching hands while he crossed to the hearth. Livvy looked up as he approached, and her brows lifted slightly as she watched him.

"How's your leg?" he asked.

She hesitated. "Sore, but at least I'm warming up."

Mason moved one of the chairs closer and sat down. "Put the heel of your foot on your chair, then wedge the rice bag against your calf. It will be hot at first, but then it will work its magic."

"Sounds very scientific," Livvy said, bending forward to take off her boot.

Mason blinked when he saw the type of socks she was wearing. "Uh, are those unicorn socks? Please tell me they are at least wool."

Livvy's cheeks pinked. "Not wool. I have a double layer of socks on."

"Take off your other boot," Mason said, shrugging out of his down coat. "And tuck both of your heels on the chair."

Livvy didn't argue and unlaced her other boot. Yep, both unicorn socks.

"Here." He handed over the rice bag.

Livvy took the rice bag and wedged it between the calf and thigh of her folded leg. "I feel like a kid sitting on a too-big chair."

Mason draped his coat over her legs. "The heat from the rice bag will warm up your legs and feet a lot faster with the coat acting as an insulator." She did look like a little kid curled up on the chair.

"What are you, one of those survivalists?"

"Eagle Scout." Mason sat on the chair next to her. "But mostly it's common sense."

"Slade just told me to flex my foot," she said.

"Slade?"

"My boyfriend," she said, exasperation in her tone.

"Oh, you mean the guy who left you out in thirty-degree weather at six o'clock in the morning?"

Livvy's eyes flashed. "He's a doctor, you know. He wouldn't endanger me."

Mason stared at her. "Well, if I get sick, I'll be sure not to go to *Dr. Slade.*"

"Dr. McKinney," she corrected.

Mason shook his head. "Whatever. I don't care *who* he is; he's a complete idiot. Not only does he not know how to treat a woman, but he put you in serious danger. He should get his medical license revoked."

Instead of defending her boyfriend, Livvy's face went pale.

Had he said too much? Then he realized she was looking past him. Mason turned. Standing behind his chair was a brown-haired man with about the whitest teeth Mason had ever seen. But the man's smile wasn't friendly, it was more . . . incredulous.

"I should get my license revoked? Why?" the man, who could only be Dr. Slade McKinney, said.

Mason had been in awkward situations before, but this beat them all. He stood instantly, and sure enough, he had a few inches on the doctor. But Mason had no advantage. He'd been caught calling the guy out. And seeing the doctor face to face made Mason regret his quick judgement—well, almost.

"Hey, Liv," the doc said, looking at her now. "How are you doing? I turned around early because I was worried about you."

Mason couldn't help the scoff that came from his throat. He couldn't have held it in if he tried. He guessed it had been at least forty minutes since Mason first saw "Liv" sitting on his stone wall.

"Much better," she said in a cheerful tone. "I was waiting

outside when I met, uh, Mason, and he gave me one of those heated rice bags . . ." Her voice trailed off when she looked down at the coat spread over her.

Her tone was way too cheerful, and Mason couldn't figure out why. She should be railing on her boyfriend-slash-doctor.

The doc extended his hand toward Mason. "Okay, well, I guess I need to thank you for helping my *girlfriend*, Mason . . .?"

Unbelievable. The doctor guy was staking his territory. Why did a kind and humane deed have to have some sort of ulterior motive? "Mason Rowe." He stepped back, not able to bring himself to shake the doctor's hand. "I'll let you take it from here, doc." He spoke in a cheery tone that rivaled Livvy's.

With barely a glance at Livvy, Mason said, "Keep the coat for now. I can get it from you at the library tomorrow. Nice to meet you all." He strode away, crossing the luxurious rugs and moving around the custom leather furniture. He didn't know if Livvy worked tomorrow, or when he'd get his coat back, but he didn't need to stick around for more pleasantries.

Outside, the cold air was like the slap he needed. The wake-up call. His agent was right. He needed to focus on his writing. When he saw a woman sitting on his stone wall, he should have just let her be and not gotten involved.

Because now he had more questions than ever about Livvy Harmon, and he didn't like that doctor-boyfriend one bit. Mason shouldn't even care, because it was none of his business. He hardly knew Livvy, and so what if being around her made his pulse quicken?

It had been a couple of years since he'd dated anyone more than casually. Women quickly tired of the ups and downs of his writing days. When the days were bad, he didn't want to do anything. When the days were good, he kept writing late into the night.

But ... he'd never leave a woman stranded, like the doctor had left Livvy. Even if the lodge had been close by, she'd still been in a lot of pain.

Maybe this experience would be the turning point in their relationship. Mr. Fancy Doctor would realize how much he'd neglected his poor freezing-cold girlfriend and would put her needs before his for once.

Not that Mason could really preach because, well, he was the king of failed relationships. And as uncomfortable as it was for Mason to realize something about himself, it was true. He and the doctor had more in common than Mason would have liked. They were both selfish men when it came to relationships.

Five

Slade sat in the chair that Mason had abandoned, asking Livvy about her leg, but her mind was reeling. *Mason Rowe?* Had she heard right? *Mason Rowe.* Impossible, she decided. Completely impossible.

"I'll be right back," Livvy said, cutting off whatever Slade was saying. "I need to go to the ladies' room."

She grasped the down coat and rice bag and stretched out her legs. When she stood, remarkably, she felt only a dull ache in her calf. Without bothering with her wet boots, she made her way to the knotty alder door with the stick figure of a woman above it. Once inside the bathroom, she set the coat and rice bag on the granite counter, then pulled out her phone.

She didn't know why her fingers were trembling when she typed *Mason Rowe thriller author* into her Safari app. Thankfully she had a few bars on her phone, and within fifteen seconds she had a list of links to click. She selected what looked like a main website.

Livvy gripped the edge of the bathroom counter when Mason Rowe's picture came up. He was beardless, and the photo was black and white, but it was definitely him.

Homeless? Hardly.

Lumberjack? Definitely not.

Livvy started to laugh at her own naiveté. Her laugh quickly went from self-deprecating to uncontrollable. Tears rolled down her cheeks, and she started to hiccup. She turned on the faucet and drank some water straight out of the sink, then splashed it on her face. Looking in the mirror, she saw the image of a completely hysterical woman.

Mason Rowe had come to *her* library.

He lived in Pine Valley in a rented cabin.

He'd heated up a rice bag for her and given her his coat.

She'd been mostly snappy and rude to him. Livvy ran a hand over her face and down her neck, wishing she could redo the last couple of days. She'd read every one of Mr. Rowe's medical thrillers. Livvy had even put his book *Cut* on the library must-read-for-Halloween list last month. His writing was dark, complex, edgy, and beautiful.

Livvy placed a hand on her chest and wondered if she was about to hyperventilate. She picked up her cell phone again and called Felicity. So what if it was 7:00 a.m. on a Sunday morning? Livvy had to figure out how to deal with her shock.

Unfortunately, or fortunately for Felicity, she didn't answer.

And Livvy couldn't stay in the bathroom much longer. She inhaled. Exhaled. Closed her eyes. Tried not to think of all the things she'd said to Mason Rowe during their two encounters. What he'd said about Slade ... Ironic because Mason Rowe always thanked various doctors and medical professionals in his acknowledgments with each book.

Yes, Livvy read the acknowledgments too.

"Okay," she whispered to herself. "I can deal with this. I can be normal when I go back into the lobby and see Slade again."

Less than a minute later, Livvy left the bathroom and found Slade talking on his cell phone in the lobby. The look on his face was one that Livvy was well familiar with. Concern mixed with business. It must be the hospital.

She slowed as she approached him.

He nodded at her without really seeing her. Livvy sighed. It wasn't like she'd been planning on them hanging out at the lodge or maybe going to breakfast somewhere, but it would have been nice. Much better than trying to keep up with him on a snowy hillside. She crossed to the chair she'd sat in and picked up her beanie and gloves. She shoved them into the pockets of her coat—the one Mason Rowe had told her wasn't warm enough.

He'd been right, of course.

Then she sat and pulled on her boots. They were still wet. When she got back to her house, she'd soak in a hot bath for at least an hour, then wear her warmest slippers the rest of the day. She stood and grabbed the ski poles. There was no doubt Slade would be taking her home soon.

Slade ended his call, and by the look in his green eyes, Livvy already knew what he was going to say.

"Sorry, Liv," he said anyway. "I've got to get to the hospital. One of my regular patients was admitted. The surgeon wants to consult with me."

"It's all right," Livvy said, and surprisingly it was. She didn't feel pouty. In fact, she felt sort of relieved. She could soak in that bath, complain to Felicity, then look up everything she could find on Mason Rowe. She had his winter coat, and when he came to pick it up, she wanted to somehow redeem her idiocy. And . . . see if she could get him to do a library event.

It would be huge. He was published in dozens of languages and sold millions and . . . she had his rice bag.

Breathe, Livvy.

He'd been really nice to her, so there was a good chance that he'd agree to a library event. Or was he one of those authors who didn't make smaller public appearances? Did he have an established honorarium? Probably. But she wouldn't let her hopes fall until she could speak to him about it.

"What are you smiling about?" Slade asked as they walked out of the lobby into the cold air.

"Oh." Was she smiling? "I'm glad my charley horse is gone, I guess."

Slade nodded and grasped her free hand.

Livvy couldn't have been more surprised. Slade had never been this affectionate toward her in public. Granted, it was still early in the morning, and only the hotel personnel seemed to be around.

"I'm glad," Slade said. "I guess the rice bag helped?"

"Yep." Livvy didn't want to get onto the subject of Mason Rowe. "How was the hike?"

Slade obliged the change in topic. "Beautiful. I love the first snowfall of the year. I'm hoping to get in some skiing this year."

Since Livvy hadn't been dating Mr. Dreamy Doc last year, she said, "Do you ski a lot?"

"I always seem to be making plans to ski." He shrugged. "But you know me, patients first."

Livvy nodded. She did know that about Slade, very well in fact.

They reached the Land Rover, and Slade opened her door, then took the ski poles to the back of the SUV. Once he climbed into the driver's seat and started the engine, Livvy was shivering again. Her wet boots weren't any help, but she didn't want to put on her beanie and gloves again, so she spread the down coat over her lap.

Slade must have noticed because he cranked up the heater, then pulled out of the parking lot. "What was that Mason guy saying about me when I came into the lodge?"

Oh. "Um, he was being dramatic, I guess," she hedged. "I wouldn't worry about it."

Slade glanced over at her. "Was he hitting on you?"

"What? No." Livvy scoffed. "He was just being nice. I stopped to sit on the wall that was apparently the backyard of his cabin."

"Oh, so he's one of *those* types," Slade said, an edge in his voice.

Livvy bristled. "What do you mean?" she asked, although she could probably guess.

"You know, the silver-spoon type," he said. "I'll bet he didn't put himself through college *and* medical school, living on less than a shoestring."

"Well, he's not a doctor either." Livvy had never really argued with Slade, and she hadn't meant to sound so bratty, but Slade didn't know anything about Mason Rowe. Of course, Mason had been equally judgmental about Slade.

She was spared an answer from Slade by his ringing phone.

He used his Bluetooth to answer, and he was still on the phone with one of the nurses when he pulled up to Livvy's house. She mimed that she was okay to get out on her own.

Relief crossed his face, and Livvy grabbed her stuff and hopped out of the Land Rover.

She hurried to the front door through the fallen snow that had covered her earlier tracks. She was shivering again as she unlocked the door. Everything was dark and quiet inside; Mallory was still asleep. *Lucky.*

Livvy's phone rang, startling her in the quiet. *Felicity.* She and Felicity were both transplants to Pine Valley, and Felicity worked in the local bookshop. When Livvy had visited the bookshop one afternoon, they'd struck up an immediate friendship over a conversation about their favorite books. Even better, Felicity lived down the block, renting her grandparents' former home.

"Hi," Livvy said. "You won't believe what a mess I've made of things."

"Good or bad?" Felicity asked.

"I don't know yet." Livvy went into her bedroom and told Felicity everything, from meeting a strange lumberjack guy in the library to how she'd gotten a cramp while hiking with Slade. By the time she got to the part about finding out Mason's true identity, Felicity was laughing.

"It's not funny," Livvy insisted, but a smile had crept onto her face. "I was completely mortified . . . I mean, I called him homeless."

"Well, at least you didn't ask him if he was a lumberjack."

"True." Livvy lay back on her bed and stared up at the ceiling. "I hate to admit this, but Slade was peevish. I should be happy about that, right? Like maybe he was jealous?"

"Oh, he was jealous," Felicity said with confidence. "I'll bet you twenty bucks that he calls you later today."

"Ha. That would be a record for him." Livvy turned on her side and ran her hand over the smoothness of the yellow-and-white bedspread. "Although he did say something about Tuesday night."

"You mean you'll see him twice in the span of a week?" Felicity asked with fake mocking.

"I know, right? Maybe I needed a knight in shining armor, who happens to be a bestselling author, to wake Slade up to how fabulous I am."

"Exactly," Felicity agreed in a teasing tone. "Your doctor will propose by Thanksgiving, and you'll elope during Christmas break."

Livvy sighed. "I'd be lucky enough to get kiss number two by Thanksgiving." She'd told Felicity about their first kiss, and both women had swooned over it, but now with the passage of time, it was all a little less swoony.

"Oh, wow," Felicity suddenly said.

"What?" Livvy sat up on her bed.

"I just looked up Mason Rowe's website, and all I can say is *mm-hmm.*"

Livvy rubbed her forehead. "He's good-looking if you like the lumberjack type."

"And since you're set on pale-faced, hiking-loving, white-toothed doctors, I'll leave you to your pursuits," Felicity said.

Livvy groaned. "Slade's and my relationship might be moving slower than a snail race, but he's not pale-faced—at least not vampire-pale."

Felicity laughed. "Well, let me know if lumberjack man shows up at the library tomorrow. If nothing else, you know where he lives."

"Yeah, I do." Livvy rose from her bed; it was time to start the bath water. "I just hope that if I apologize sufficiently, he'll agree to do a library event."

"I'm betting another twenty bucks that he'll say yes."

Six

By the time Mason had shoveled snow from the cabin's driveway, he'd had enough of a workout to skip going to the gym in town. He'd only been there once, and he already missed his usual running route in mild San Diego.

The skies were clear and ice blue this morning, and Mason had no excuse not to get to the library. Yesterday had been another dud. No writing. Well, he'd written a paragraph, then deleted it. He'd shut his laptop before he could start revising the twelve pages his agent was so proud of, which he'd typed up from his handwritten pages.

As Mason put away the snow shovel, then went into the cabin to grab his keys and notepad, he thought of his main character, an unassuming and newly injured football player who would soon become caught up in an illegal prescription cartel. Mason had written enough in the genre that he didn't need to do much research. But he was always thorough, so it would be nice to ask a doctor a few questions.

He hadn't forged any personal relationships outside San Diego, and now he was regretting his curt words about Dr. Slade McKinney. Mason had taken a few minutes to look up the Pine Valley Hospital and found that Dr. McKinney was a primary physician both at the hospital and with his own private practice.

Mason supposed he could google some information on how patients were able to duplicate prescriptions and forge insurance cards, but he always prided himself on getting things accurate. He didn't relish speaking with a pharmacist because they tended to be very close-minded and suspicious. Doctors were more objective.

Well, Dr. McKinney certainly wasn't the only doctor in this small town.

Mason fired up his Jeep and drove into town. After grabbing a bagel and coffee at the Main Street Café, he headed to the library. He hadn't realized how keyed up he was to see Olivia Harmon—Livvy—until he saw that the librarian on duty was another woman. The strawberry-blonde lady greeted him with a friendly welcome, and when he said he didn't need help finding anything, she turned back to the computer she'd been browsing on.

Okay then.

Maybe Livvy would come in later. It wasn't like he was in a big hurry to get his coat and rice bag back. In fact, she could keep the bag. He didn't have any real outdoor plans save for future shoveling—and he quickly became too hot to wear a coat anyway.

Mason found the same table he'd worked at before and took a seat. It was next to the floor-to-ceiling windows and afforded him a majestic view of the ski resort. The library architecture was impressive, a work of art in and of itself.

Mason hadn't ripped off the previous pages from the

notepad, so he skimmed through them, catching himself up on the plot and beginnings of characterization. The football player's name was Pilot, a nickname, but for a good reason. Not only was he a star quarterback, but he was a natural leader, which would be important to his character arc later in the story.

Now to think of the name of the doctor who'd first prescribe a large quantity of opioids to Pilot. *Dr. Slade McKinney?* No. Depending on how long Mason stayed in Pine Valley to write, he might get to know a few people, and those people would likely read this book. *Dr. Sloane Mackinley.* Close, yet different. And it would be fun to make the doctor character the first level of corruption that Pilot would encounter.

Mason began to write, setting the scene of the doctor's office and getting inside Pilot's point of view. Describing his pain, noticing what he noticed, his first impressions of the doctor, and the moment when Pilot questioned the prescription.

Before Mason knew it, an hour had passed, and he'd written four pages.

What if he set the injury event right before the football team's bowl game so that it was the last game of the year . . . Pilot would sit on the sidelines, watching as the second-string quarterback got all the minutes.

Fourth quarter, two and a half minutes left, first down, and the second string throws a wild pass. Pilot downs two of the pills he brought with him, then he tells the coach to put him in. At first the coach refuses, then finally agrees to one play.

Pilot jogs onto the field to the cheers of the fans, and he can feel the drugs doing their work. He's invincible. He throws a touchdown to tie the game, then throws a two-point conversion. He runs down the rest of the minutes on the clock, and his team wins. Pilot knows that whatever the doctor gave him, there was no doubt that it had been the difference between winning and losing.

Mason's hand started to ache, but the words kept coming. He hardly noticed if someone came and sat in the library or if someone left. A young mom brought in her two little kids, but their noise didn't even bother Mason.

Finally he had to take a bathroom break, and he set down his pen. The ornate clock above the bookcase across from him read 1:00 p.m. Mason had been writing for four straight hours. He stood and picked up the notebook to find he'd written fifteen pages. Two complete scenes and more ideas were tumbling through his mind.

Jolene was going to throw a party.

Mason found the bathroom, then drank from the drinking fountain. His stomach wasn't satisfied with just water, but he didn't want to break up his momentum. On his way back to his table by the windows, he slowed his step. The strawberry-blonde librarian was gone, and the woman who was now behind the reference desk was undoubtedly the dark-haired Livvy Harmon.

She wore a pale-green scarf in her hair, sort of like a headband, so that her dark curls were smoothed from her forehead.

Livvy looked up just then, and their gazes connected. He smiled, but instead of an answering smile in return, she frowned.

Talk about a punch to the gut. *Okay then.* He walked toward his table, not looking back, and by the time he sat down, he wondered why he even cared. If she had his coat, she knew he was there and could bring it over. Maybe she'd been mad about what he'd said about her boyfriend, but it was true. Slade McKinney *was* an idiot.

Mason picked up his notebook and pen, then reread the last few paragraphs. Pilot was celebrating with his teammates, accepting credit for something he knew was artificial. But that was okay, Pilot reasoned. He was a great player; he had just needed a little help. Plus, if the second-string quarterback had stayed in, their team would have lost. A couple of extra pills was a very small price to pay.

Mason thought about where the turning point would be for Pilot—that time when he realized he was addicted and couldn't go even a few hours without his pills.

And then Mason thought about Livvy and why she'd frowned at him. What was her problem? He thought small towns were all about hospitality—but it seemed he'd been dead wrong—

Back to the story, he commanded himself. If the season was over, then Pilot would likely take some sort of holiday before winter training started up again. Maybe he goes on a ski trip and wants to impress a few ladies at the resort. So Pilot overdoes it, ends up going through the rest of his prescription lightning fast—

Livvy Harmon might be a pretty woman, but personality went a long way in Mason's opinion. Besides, the woman had a boyfriend—a doctor, no less—lame as he was. Jolene had been right. No distractions—

"Mr. Rowe?" someone said behind him.

It was Livvy's voice. Strange that Mason already recognized it. He turned his head, not bothering to shift his chair or anything. She could come around the table if she wanted more of his attention.

"Do you have a minute?" she asked. "Or am I interrupting?"

"I'm just writing," Mason said, setting his pen down.

"Oh." Livvy's eyes rounded, and she didn't move.

Mason sighed. Why did he have to do all the work here? "I have a minute."

"Okay, great." Her voice was a notch higher now. She pulled out the chair right next to him and sat in it.

Well, there was nowhere to look but at her. She smelled of cinnamon, and she looked decidedly warmer. Not the half-frozen woman he'd encountered yesterday morning. "How's your leg?" he asked, not intending to be the one to carry the conversation—but it was too late to take his question back.

She didn't frown, so he supposed that was a good sign.

"Completely better, thanks to you," she said, her expression still quite somber.

He tried not to gaze at the freckle above her mouth or notice how her sweater was the same color as the scarf. Or think of how her nose wasn't pink from the cold and how she was no longer shivering.

She clasped her hands atop the table. "I owe you an apology."

This was not what he had expected her to say. Maybe something more along the lines of *Get lost and don't ever insult my boyfriend, aka the doctor, again.* "For what?"

"For accusing you of being homeless and then not properly thanking you for your help on Sunday, and of course, for not welcoming you to Pine Valley. And for not realizing that you're a famous author." She took a breath. "We're usually more hospitable to new residents, or visitors, or whatever it is you are."

He felt like laughing, although she wasn't trying to be funny. And he wouldn't consider himself "famous." He didn't have a movie or Netflix series based on any of his books, which was the pinnacle for every author. "I'm a visitor."

"Visitor," she repeated.

Her eyelashes were long, and this close up, he noticed that her eyes weren't simply brown. There was some evidence of gold, making them tawny brown. That was a pretty good detail to notice. *Tawny brown.* He should use that in his manuscript. Not for Pilot, of course. Maybe for the nurse that Pilot would meet when he went back for a follow-up appointment to get another refillable prescription.

Wow. Mason mentally shook his head. This manuscript was really digging its claws into him, taking hold of his psyche. That was a very good sign. Although he'd written fifteen pages today, he could write at least that much more. But right now, librarian Livvy Harmon was watching him with a confused expression. He wondered if she knew she had tiny lines between her eyebrows when she did that.

"Where did you go?" she asked.

"What?" He had no idea what she was talking about.

"You . . ." She waved a hand, as if to include the whole of him in her explanation. "You looked like you were having an entire conversation in your head."

He thought about this. "You're probably right. The color of your eyes made me think of something I should put in my book."

Her gaze cut to the notepad on the table. "Is that what you're doing in the library? *Writing a book?*"

"Uh, yes?" Was it so strange to write in a library? Reading and writing sounded like very common activities in a place like this.

Livvy pressed a hand to her heart. "Is it the sequel to *Cut,* or another standalone?"

All right, this was unexpected. "You've read my books?"

When her gaze returned to his, he saw the glimmer in her eyes. *Oh no.* He didn't want *this* from her—the admiration that a fan might have—which he'd encountered plenty of times. He'd enjoyed Livvy the woman, not Livvy the fan.

"I've read all of your books," she gushed.

Seven

Why Mason Rowe didn't look particularly pleased, or even impressed, when she told him she'd read all his books, she didn't know. Wasn't that what authors wanted to hear from their fans? That they'd purchased every new release and devoured it in two days?

Yet those blue eyes of his weren't exactly thrilled.

"I'm sorry, I don't mean to freak you out," she said. "I should probably let you get back to . . . writing." Her voice had become breathless—did he notice it? He'd probably think she was an author stalker now. Was there such a term? But before she could put the appropriate distance between them, she rushed ahead with the rest of her questions. "How long will you be in Pine Valley? And would you consider doing an event at the library? Maybe a reading of *Cut,* then a Q&A? We could do it Thanksgiving weekend as sort of our own Black Friday event. I could even order books for a signing."

Mason put his hand on her arm, and she closed her mouth.

"I'll talk to my agent," he said. "She's pretty stressed right now about this manuscript. I missed the submission deadline, and I'm only now making progress. My agent doesn't want any distractions from the outside world, thus why I'm here in Pine Valley living in a rented cabin."

His hand was still on her arm. "I get it," Livvy said, and she did. She wasn't a writer herself, but when she read a book, she sometimes became so involved, she gave up sleep to finish.

Mason continued. "But I'm not sure if my agent would consider a library event a distraction. Although if there are rabid fans around, it could become harder to write at the library."

One side of his mouth had lifted into a smile, and she didn't know if he was teasing her. Or if he was implying that *she* was acting the part of the rabid fan.

Well, she'd own it. "Okay, I can wait to hear what your agent says. But I want you to know that I started reading your books when you had three or four out. I've always been fascinated with the medical field. Your books have just the right amount of suspense and medical stuff combined. I also like that your books have all been stand-alone reads so far even though you've created your own trope of main characters being injured athletes."

He lifted his hand from her arm and rubbed the back of his neck. "There are pros and cons to carving out a niche in a genre," he said. "I feel pigeon-holed sometimes. Yet when I get into the characters I'm writing about, I always find new angles. So I'm not bored yet." He gave her a lazy smile.

Okay, so Livvy was getting used to the beard. That didn't mean she found it attractive, but like Felicity had pointed out, even a beard couldn't take away from the handsomeness that was Mason Rowe. Had he become *more* handsome after Livvy had found out that he was a bestselling thriller writer?

She swallowed. "Well, I for one love your books. Do you always write at libraries?"

"This is my first," he said with a shrug. "But it seems to be working. I've written more in the past few days than I have in an entire year."

"Oh, that's great news, right?" She straightened. Maybe when Mason Rowe left Pine Valley, she'd put a little plaque on this table declaring that he'd written his book here. "What's this book about?"

He shifted. "So, here's the thing," he said in low tone. "I don't discuss my works in progress when I'm drafting, not even with my agent."

This surprised Livvy. "Never?"

"Never."

"Is it bad karma or something?" she asked. "Like how Jackson had superstitious habits in *Slice*?"

His gaze looked amused. "All baseball players have those types of superstitions."

"And you were a basketball player in college, right?"

"Right."

Again she had the feeling he was laughing at her. She was a librarian, and she did have a good memory, and she did read a lot of books. Not only his. She wouldn't admit that she'd read most of his books twice. And it didn't seem like he was going to elaborate on his basketball-playing years. She should make herself scarce, let him get back to whatever top-secret manuscript he was writing.

She wanted to ask him if he always drafted by hand, but she'd probably worn out her welcome. Sliding back her chair, she rose. "Thanks for talking to me, and thanks for everything else too. Let me know what your agent says, and if you can't do an event, no worries."

His gaze had followed her as she stood. "I'll let you know," he said.

"Oh, and I'll go grab your coat and rice bag right now," she said. "I should have brought them over in the first place."

The amused gleam in his eyes was back, which only made her feel foolish. She hurried off, hoping that he wasn't watching her. She wouldn't be surprised if she tripped. Why was she feeling so antsy and nervous around him? Oh yeah. He was a major bestselling author, and he was writing his *next book in her library!*

Breathe, Livvy. She moved behind the reference desk, took a guzzle from her still-cold water bottle, then picked up the coat and rice bag she'd brought with her. Felicity would get a kick out of the conversation Livvy had just had with Mason Rowe. But Livvy wouldn't be telling her friend *everything*, not how he'd touched her arm (for kind of a long time) or how she'd noticed his scent—clean soap and something else more musky and masculine.

She should be thinking of how *Slade* smelled. He always smelled clean too—antiseptic clean, that was, with maybe a dash of spicy cologne on their dates. As she returned to Mason's designated table, Livvy thought of how much she loved Slade's easy smile and how he cared so much for his patients—as individuals, not as clients. If she hadn't cramped up on their hike yesterday, and if Mason Rowe hadn't gotten in the middle of everything, Slade probably would have kissed her again. And their second kiss would be longer and more fulfilling.

It was with this happy and hopeful thought that she swept quietly past Mason Rowe and deposited his down coat and rice bag without a sound in the chair next to him, so that she didn't disturb his writing. Although he wasn't exactly writing.

He was mostly staring at a blank page, fiddling with the pen in his hand.

Still, he was probably right in the middle of a scene in his head.

She moved away, not wanting to break his concentration, when he suddenly said, "It's good to see you appropriately dressed for the library."

She stopped and turned. He was leaning back in his chair, notebook and pen still in his hands, but his eyes were no longer on the blank page. Instead, he was looking at her . . . quite intently, in fact. Was he checking her out?

She wasn't dressed to impress really. Well, she had known there was a good chance of seeing one of her favorite thriller writers today. So she'd worn her jeans that were dark and newer, which made them more dressy in her opinion, and she'd chosen the pale-green sweater and head scarf that people always complimented her on. "I have no trouble dressing for indoor activities."

Mason Rowe smiled at her.

Really smiled.

Like heart-stopping.

Before Livvy could gather her wits and wonder what in the world her heart was thinking, Mason pushed back his chair and stood.

"You're done?" she quipped, then regretted her question. It was none of her business.

"Not sure. All I know is that I'm too hungry to focus." He glanced at the library clock. "I've been here since opening."

It was after 2:00 p.m. now. "We have a stash of granola bars." What was she thinking? "I mean, you probably need more sustenance than that, being so tall and—" *Shut up now, Livvy.*

Mason chuckled and picked up his notepad and pen.

Then he was walking toward her . . . well, he *would* have to pass her to get to the library exit.

"Thanks," he said, pausing by her. "That's a nice offer, but I think I'll pass on the granola bars."

Livvy looked up at him because he was standing fairly close. "Okay."

His blue eyes connected with hers. "You're an interesting woman, Livvy Harmon. Maybe I'll see you tomorrow."

She could only nod and watch him continue on his way to the library exit. He'd been . . . complimentary? Nice? *Flirty?* Livvy grasped the top of a nearby chair, if only to keep herself grounded and her thoughts realistic. He didn't wear a wedding ring, and there'd been no mention of a wife or kids in his website bio, but that didn't mean much. He might just be a private person. He didn't even share his book's plot with his agent when he was writing.

You're an interesting woman, Livvy Harmon, he'd said. Who said that in real life? Apparently Mason Rowe did, but his life wasn't typical, she guessed. What would it be like to make up stories for a living, then have millions of people buy them? And what had he meant by "interesting"—was that *good* interesting or *weird* interesting?

Maybe I'll see you tomorrow. So did that mean he was coming to the library again in the morning? Livvy's schedule was usually the later one, from noon to close, and Mallory took the mornings. What if he was gone before Livvy arrived at work?

Her cell phone buzzed as she walked back to the reference desk. She pulled it from her pocket, half expecting the text to be from Felicity, or maybe Mallory. They were going to get together and make pizza from scratch tonight. Her steps slowed when she saw that Slade had texted her: *Hey, Liv. Are you free tonight? My last appointment should be over by 5:30 and I thought I could make up that cancelled dinner date to you.*

Livvy stared at the words for a full minute before she could process them. Then, because it would be at least forty-five minutes before the school kids started to show up at the library, she called Felicity, hoping her friend could answer.

"Did he text you?" Felicity said as soon as she picked up her phone.

"How did you know?" Livvy asked.

"You never call me during work hours," Felicity said with a laugh. "So I figured if you were calling instead of texting, then Slade had done something earth-shattering."

Livvy sat on the chair behind the reference desk. "He wants to take me out to dinner. *Tonight.*"

"Wow."

"I know, *wow.*"

"I guess you'll be missing pizza night, but I'm sure you'd rather eat gourmet Italian with Slade," Felicity said.

For the first time in, well, ever, she regretted that Slade had made time for her. She'd been looking forward to hanging out with her friends, laughing, and eating until they were stuffed. Livvy shook those thoughts away. *Of course* she wanted to go out with Slade.

"You and Mallory will have to survive without me," Livvy said in a bright tone.

Felicity laughed. "Admit it, you're already thinking of your next kiss with Slade."

No. She wasn't. She was wondering if Slade really wanted to make up the cancelled date, or if he was just annoyed with the attention she'd gotten from Mason Rowe. As usual, Felicity seemed to read her mind.

"Slade likes you, Livvy," she said. "Mr. Hot Thriller

Writer or not, Slade has been dating you for months. If it takes another man's attention to get Slade to step up his game, then it's a win-win for both of you."

Livvy sighed. "You're right, and you're also creepily observant."

"I'll take it as a compliment," Felicity said, a smile sounding in her voice. "By the way, I downloaded *Cut* to my Kindle and read a few chapters this morning."

"What did you think?" Livvy asked.

"Uh, a little too dark for me," she said.

"You have to keep reading," Livvy said. "You won't be able to put it down once you get to chapter five."

"I think I'll stick with my fantasy novels and romances," Felicity said. "But I put in an order for all of his books for the bookshop. Five titles of each release. If you think he might agree to do a book signing, I can get more in."

Livvy explained how she'd already extended the invitation, albeit in a more expansive way, and how he had said he was under a strict deadline.

Felicity was quiet for a moment after Livvy stopped talking. So quiet that Livvy checked her connection.

"Did a customer come in?" Livvy pressed.

"I was just thinking," Felicity said. "Maybe we should invite Mason to pizza night tonight. I mean, he probably needs to eat sometime, and it would be good for him to get to know the citizens of Pine Valley."

"You wouldn't dare," Livvy said.

"Ha!" Felicity scoffed. "I knew it."

"Knew *what*?" Livvy asked.

"Never mind," Felicity said, triumph in her voice. "I'd better get back to work. Call me after your date with Slade—I want a full report."

Felicity hung up, and Livvy was left wondering why it had made her feel *jealous* when Felicity suggested inviting Mason to pizza night.

Eight

Mason was starting to hate snow.

If only he'd hit his deadline when he was supposed to, he wouldn't be in Pine Valley, shoveling another six inches of snow from a rented cabin's driveway. Apparently there was a snow removal service for the cabins, but it didn't come until after Mason wanted to leave for the day.

So Mason pulled on his boots, gloves, and hat and trudged outside. He supposed the falling snow was picturesque, but there was definitely truth in how too much of a good thing sort of spoiled itself.

Mason wasn't asking for much, and over the past couple of weeks, his routine had been simple.

Wake early, go to the Pine Valley Recreation Center. Run the track, lift weights, shower, change, eat breakfast at the Main Street Café, then he'd write at the library until he was hungry for lunch. He was writing slower than he ever had in his career, but at least he was writing, averaging ten to fifteen pages a day. And Jolene was more than pleased with his progress.

Yesterday he'd reached page 120, and the first turn, or climax, was about to occur. Mason decided if he could get his usual fifteen pages written today, he'd do something to celebrate. Maybe go see a movie? He could watch movies as long as they weren't in the same genre he was writing. He didn't want to get ideas that would influence his current work in progress.

Driveway and walkway finished, Mason peeled off his gloves and hat in the house, changed his boots, then grabbed his gym bag. He climbed into his Jeep, shivering until the interior warmed up. He took the canyon road slowly. Even though the snowplows had made at least one pass this morning, the snow was coming down pretty good now.

By the time he pulled up to the rec center, he couldn't even see the lines to park. Whoever had plowed the parking lot would have to make a return visit soon. Making his best estimate, he pulled into a space, then climbed out. The snow seemed to have kept quite a few people away, since the parking lot was about half its usual fullness.

He hurried inside and went straight to the track, which was a floor above the basketball gym. He wasn't even tempted to join in any of the pickup games. His father had been his high school basketball coach, and Mason had spent years of his life trying to make the old man happy. His father had since passed away now, but the tightening of Mason's gut still happened whenever he was around the game.

Which was ironic, he knew, because he continued to write medical thrillers with athletes as central characters.

He ran for about an hour, then hit the weight room. It seemed things had picked up at the gym, and more than half the machines were being used. While he waited his turn for one of the machines, a tall man with blond hair struck up a conversation.

"I've seen you here a few times," the man said. "Are you new to Pine Valley or on a long vacation?"

"I'm renting a cabin at the resort," Mason said. "Working on a deadline."

At the man's interested expression, Mason added, "I'm a writer."

"Oh? Who do you work for?" the man continued.

"Myself. I write novels." Mason knew from experience that he'd get one of two reactions. The person would be impressed and ask a ton of questions. Or the person would politely say, "How interesting. I guess you have the easy job, chasing a muse all day." Or something like that.

But this man did neither. "You must be Mason Rowe, then. I heard you were in town. I should have put two and two together."

Who was talking about him? Mason wondered. His only personal interaction had been with the town librarian, but maybe that had been enough. Was she telling other people? Or maybe she was dating this guy too?

"I'm Dawson Harris," the man said, sticking out his hand.

"Well, apparently you know who I am." Mason shook his hand, keeping it brief, because they were in a gym. Sweating. Before he could ask Dawson Harris how he'd heard of him, Dawson spoke.

"If you need a lawyer again, then I'm your guy." Dawson leaned closer and lowered his voice. "Read about that nasty lawsuit. If I'd been on the case, it wouldn't have gone past the discovery stage."

Mason couldn't have been more surprised that this man knew about the lawsuit, and that he'd have the nerve to criticize the case. Mason moved back a few inches, marking his distance. "Who told you I was in Pine Valley?"

Dawson frowned, then his face relaxed. "Oh, it was Slade. I ran into him the other day—he's Dr. McKinney now—and he asked me if I knew anything about your legal case. I didn't, but I looked it up on the spot. Slade informed me that you were in town and said you'd helped out his girlfriend at the ski resort or something."

Mason could only reply, "Yes."

"I thought it was strange that he was so interested in some visitor to Pine Valley," Dawson said. "Now that I see you, I can understand his concern."

Mason blinked. "*Concern*?"

"Slade said his girlfriend is pretty much obsessed with you." He shrugged. "Not in the stalker way—of course—but she's always talking about your books, and how she can't believe you're writing your next book in her library. I guess it's making Slade concerned."

Mason had to clench his jaw to keep his mouth from falling open in astonishment. He'd talked to Livvy almost every day, but their conversations were brief, and she kept to her end of the library, and he kept to his. But . . . if Mason were to guess, Slade was the dramatic type. He seemed to enjoy extremes. Extreme hiking, ignoring his girlfriend to the extreme, and now asking other people in Pine Valley if they knew Mason.

Unbelievable. "How is Livvy's interest in my work a concern to the doctor, or to *you*, for that matter?"

Dawson didn't seem fazed by the question at all. In fact, he laughed. "Let's just say that if you were about thirty years older and missing a couple of teeth, Slade would be sleeping better at night. As it is, Slade would prefer that you hold your writing sessions someplace other than the library. But if you ask me, stay right where you are. Slade needs a little competition. Livvy is way too beautiful and sassy to be strung along month after month."

Mason *really* didn't like Slade McKinney. Not when he'd first met him, and not now. According to this Dawson character, Livvy was being *strung along.* What exactly did that mean? Mason scrubbed a hand over his beard. "Next time you see the doc, tell him I'm happy to autograph a book for him any time. His girlfriend knows where to find me." Mason turned and walked to the next open machine on the other side of the room.

Dawson didn't follow him, and when Mason next looked up, the man had left the room.

Good. Mason didn't need any small-town lawyer, or doctor, telling him what he could and couldn't do.

Mason probably lifted a little longer than usual, and more weight than typical, which would make him plenty sore by the end of the day. But it felt good to work off the annoyance that was Dawson Harris—or more accurately, Slade McKinney. Doctor or not, the guy needed a wake-up call. Because no woman should ever be strung along, and Mason was determined to figure out what Dawson had meant.

No, Mason wouldn't go so far as asking Livvy out on a date, but it wouldn't hurt to flirt with her a little, would it? Give the doc a run for his money? Of course, Mason had been flirting with Livvy already—in a completely prosaic way. Both he and Livvy knew that she was a fan of his writing, and he didn't mind some encouragement and a few compliments. Completely innocent.

Although Slade McKinney didn't know that.

Mason found that he was smiling by the time he'd showered and dressed in the locker room. He happened to know that Livvy was working the morning shift today, so what would it hurt if he brought her breakfast? Friends did that, right? And what was wrong with him and Livvy becoming better friends?

When Mason reached the library, it was open, but only one car was in the parking lot. He assumed the red Honda Accord belonged to Livvy. He wasn't surprised to see that her car was red. He grabbed the sack of muffins and bagels he'd bought since he didn't know which she liked, then tucked his notebook under his arm and balanced two cups of hot coffee as he walked to the front doors.

He managed to open the heavy doors with a spare finger, then he walked through the lobby, ignoring the *No Food, No Drinks Please* sign.

Livvy looked up from the reference desk as he approached. She smiled as their gazes met, then lines appeared between her brows when she noticed that he was carrying food.

"Don't kick me out before you hear what I've come to say," Mason said.

She folded her arms and tilted her head. "All right." She wore a long-sleeved, black V-neck shirt that made her hair look even darker and her eyes almost black. Her curly hair was piled on top of her head in a sort of messy bun, and she wore long, dangling silver earrings.

And she smelled . . . great. Like cinnamon and sugar. Or maybe that was the breakfast. He set the sack on the counter that separated him from her.

"They had a two-for-one deal at the café," he said, "so I thought I'd bring you breakfast."

She rested her hands on the counter and leaned forward to peer into the bag he'd opened. Yep. She smelled great.

"Oooh, I love the blueberry muffins."

"Perfect, because that's exactly what I got for you." Mason pulled the muffin out of the sack and set it on a napkin.

"Sure you did." Livvy smiled and slid the napkin toward her. "You know, this is breaking all kinds of rules."

"I know." He winked. "Coffee?"

"Yes, thanks," she said. "I didn't sleep too great last night, and I'll start to feel it soon."

"Up reading all night?" Mason teased.

"Not exactly," she said, then shrugged. "I think I'm just excited for tonight?"

Mason lifted his brows and waited.

"I'm going on a date with Slade."

"Ah." Mason tried not to reveal the stab of disappointment he felt. "You must really like this guy to lose sleep over a date."

She looked away and didn't say anything.

This confused him. Shouldn't she be gushing over her doctor-boyfriend? "Unless you're . . . dreading it?"

Her gaze snapped to his, her eyes wide. "I'm not dreading it. I mean, Slade has asked me out more than usual since . . . since, ever."

Mason studied her ~~brown~~ eyes, her pert nose, the dusty pink of her lips, that freckle. "More than usual. What does that mean?"

"Well, we used to go out every couple of weeks," she said in a slow tone. "Because of his schedule, you know, being a doctor and all."

He knew.

"But after that day hiking, where I ran into you, he started calling and texting every day," she said. "He's been really sweet, I suppose, but I'm not used to all the attention. In fact, I used to complain to my friend Felicity about not spending enough time with him."

"And now it's too much?" Mason surmised.

She looked down at her coffee cup. "Not too much. I mean, he's my boyfriend, and there's no such thing as too much."

Mason didn't say anything for a moment. "Maybe he finally realized what he's got."

Her brown eyes studied him. "I'd like to think that, but I don't feel that."

Mason leaned against the counter, which brought him a few inches closer to her. "Maybe . . . he's making sure you're staying busy. Did you ever think of that?"

She blinked. "You mean he's doing more stuff with me so that I don't do other stuff?"

"Yeah."

"What would the *other* stuff be?" she said. "I'm a boring person. I work at a library all day, and I have like three friends."

"Three?"

"Mallory, Felicity, and . . ." She stared at him innocently. "Me?"

She laughed. "Sure, why not?"

Mason smiled. "I'm glad I'm your friend, but I'm also a bit worried about what that might entail."

Her brows darted upward. "Why's that?"

"I think your boyfriend is territorial, and I can't say I blame him," Mason said. "His buddy Dawson Harris talked to me this morning at the gym. And let's just say it wasn't a friendly conversation."

"Wow." Livvy folded her arms. "Slade's asked a lot of questions about you, and he thinks it's strange that you're at the library so much when you have an entire cabin to yourself. I tried to explain how the muse works, and even though I'm not a writer, I sort of get it."

So it was Slade who was garnering information from Livvy, and not her telling Slade all about Mason. "I think my first impression of your doctor still stands."

Livvy sighed. "Slade is an amazing guy, but I don't know what's got into him. Felicity thinks he jealous, but that doesn't make sense. I mean, there's nothing going on between you and me, so there's nothing for Slade to worry about."

Mason looked down at the cup of coffee on the counter, then back up at her. "I don't want to get in the middle of your relationship, but why does it take the attentions of another man to get your boyfriend to spend more time with you?" By the look on her face, Mason knew he'd gone too far. But it was too late to take it back now.

Livvy dropped her arms and rested her hands on the counter. "That's what I was wondering too."

Nine

Of course a novelist would be observant and have that added insight into the psyche of people, aka characters. So why was Livvy surprised when Mason had seen right through her relationship with Slade and voiced all her fears with a few simple questions? All right, she wasn't surprised. Anyone, best-selling author or not, would be able to figure out what was going on.

Slade was staking his territory, and his territory was her. Slade's comments about Mason Rowe had been derogatory, and Mason's comments had been . . . critical.

But for some reason, Livvy found that she was agreeing with Mason a lot more than Slade. Which was dangerous, and which should probably tell her something.

No. No. No.

She didn't want to think of a future without Slade. They'd been dating for *months,* and he was her ideal man. Successful. Handsome. Intelligent. Respected. The man she'd been dreaming of for as long as she could remember.

71

And he liked *her*, right? He'd kissed her that one time, and he'd held her hand on every date now. Still not a second kiss, but Livvy was trying not to let that bother her.

At some point, Mason had left the food on the counter, taking only one of the coffee cups. He'd gone to his seat at his usual table, and Livvy didn't even remember telling him thank you or wishing him a good writing session.

No one else had come into the library, and the silence felt deafening with just the two of them inside the building. Of course, with irony she thought of how annoyed Slade would be with the fact that she was essentially alone with Mason and that they'd had breakfast together.

She finished the muffin and stashed the sack beneath the counter. Then she carried her coffee cup over to Mason's table. He wasn't actually writing but tapping his pen against the notebook. He looked up when she sat across from him, his blue eyes connecting with hers.

"So," she said. "I think I should explain something."

"You don't owe me *any* explanations," he said in a low tone. "I shouldn't be butting in."

"Well, that's true." She offered a smile, but his expression remained sober. "When you asked why I couldn't sleep last night, I think it was because I'm worried that Slade is paying more attention to me now because of you."

Mason nodded. "He thinks I'm some sort of threat."

"Which you're not," she was quick to say.

"Which I'm not," he deadpanned.

Her pulse sped up. "Now that *would* make things complicated." She laughed, and it came out a nervous sound.

"Beyond complicated," Mason said. "I don't even live here."

"And you probably have a girlfriend, or two, in San Diego," Livvy said in a more determined tone. "You're a successful author, a dang good writer, a kind person, and a nice-looking guy too, despite the beard."

"I don't have a girlfriend, and especially not *two.*" Mason set his pen down and shifted forward on his chair. His blue eyes seemed to bore into her. "I appreciate all the compliments, but what's wrong with the beard?"

Heat flashed through Livvy. Had she really brought up his beard? "Nothing, I mean, it's fine. I'm not a beard person, but that doesn't matter because—" She cut herself off.

His eyes glinted with humor. "Because . . . ?"

"Because there's nothing between us anyway," she said. "So it doesn't matter to me whether you choose to look like a grizzly bear."

Mason's eyes widened, then he dropped his face into his hands and laughed.

And kept laughing. Livvy was glad no one was in the library because he was breaking the *Keep Quiet Please* rule. After perhaps a full minute, she said, "Are you finished yet?"

He only laughed some more, and when he lifted his head, he wiped at the tears on his face.

"All right, I guess I'm glad I could be your entertainment for the morning." She rose to her feet. "Thanks for breakfast by the way."

He was still laughing when she walked back to the reference counter. Eventually he stopped, and Livvy guessed he'd finally started writing again because there were no more sounds from his corner of the library.

When lunch time neared, she opted for the extra bagel in the bag instead of the wilted turkey sandwich she'd brought. She'd kept away from Mason's corner and hadn't even spied on him—which she'd done plenty of times in the past. So she was surprised when a group of school kids came into the library. It was that late already?

Mallory would be arriving soon as well, and still Livvy hadn't ventured over to Mason.

She was straightening up after showing a couple of sixth graders how to use one of the computers when Mason appeared.

"I hit a record today," he said without any preamble.

"Oh?"

He held up his notebook. "Twenty pages."

Livvy smiled. "Wow, that's great. Your agent will be ecstatic." They'd talked enough about his agent that Livvy knew Mason had to check in at the end of each day and report on his progress.

"Want to celebrate?" Mason asked.

Livvy's stomach nearly flipped over. He was asking her *out*? Or was it more like . . . coffee? "I've got plans tonight with Slade, remember?"

The blue of his eyes darkened a fraction—or maybe it was her imagination. Was it also her imagination that he looked disappointed?

"Right," he said. "See you tomorrow, Livvy Harmon."

"See you . . ." Her voice trailed off as he turned. "And Mason?" she called after him, as loud as she dared.

He paused and glanced back.

"I think that's fantastic."

Mason nodded, and although he didn't smile, his blue eyes had lightened again.

She had to force herself not to call him back while she watched him walk to the library exit alone. He'd had a great writing day, and she'd turned down his offer of celebrating with him. Maybe she could cancel on Slade, and then call Mason and tell him she was free. Yet what would she tell Slade? And . . . she didn't have Mason's phone number.

She was still debating, still regretting, when Mallory arrived.

"A quiet day, huh?" Mallory said. She wore her strawberry-blonde hair in a thick braid.

Only a handful of people occupied the library. "This is the most busy it's been," Livvy said, anxious to be on her way. She wanted to think through everything without any distractions. So she explained to Mallory what needed to be done, then she hurried out of the library.

The snow had piled up like crazy on her car, and she took several minutes to get it cleared off enough to drive. By the time she got inside the car, her hands were numb from pushing off the snow. On the drive home, she drove like an inchworm on the slushy roads. She couldn't get rid of the image of Mason leaving the library alone.

Maybe tomorrow she could bring him a treat or something. She could get a couple of those gourmet cupcakes. She had to admit she didn't know what he liked to eat or what he liked for dessert. There was so much she didn't know about him, yet they'd talked every day for the past two weeks at the library.

Somehow he'd been able to get her to reveal much more information about herself than the other way around.

As she pulled into her driveway, a text came from Slade. For a split second, Livvy hoped he was cancelling. She could track down Mason somehow, maybe even show up at his cabin with those cupcakes. But no, Slade had texted that he'd meet her at the movie theater since he was in back-to-back appointments. They'd eat at the taco place that was in the same parking lot at 6:30 p.m., then watch whatever was playing at 7:00. *Your choice,* Slade had texted. *Whatever you want to see.*

Livvy sighed and climbed out of her car. She went into

the quiet house and sat down on the couch, still wearing her coat. She pulled up the theater website on her phone. There was an animated movie about ants and a western-type show. Western it would be.

Livvy suddenly felt tired, and so she set her alarm for 5:30 p.m. and lay down on the couch. When it went off, she was startled awake. Apparently she really had taken a nap, and she felt even more tired than she had before she crashed.

She checked her phone. No new texts from Slade, so it seemed everything was still on for tonight. So Livvy brushed her teeth and reapplied some makeup. She added a spritz of cinnamon-vanilla body spray, then she was as ready as she wanted to be.

She thought about calling Felicity to mull over all that Mason had said to her and how Livvy was, for the first time, not too excited about seeing Slade. But she already knew what Felicity would say about Slade, and Livvy didn't want to hear it.

The taco place was packed—it seemed everyone else in Pine Valley had the same idea. Since it had started to snow again, Livvy had hoped everyone would stay home in their cozy houses. Nope.

I'm here, she texted Slade. *The taco shop is packed. Do you want to go somewhere else?*

Seconds later, Slade wrote back. *Wait in line. I should be leaving the office soon. If you have to order before I get there, get me the pork chimichangas and a large Vitamin Water.*

He hadn't even left the office? It was a good fifteen-minute drive in this weather. She stared at the text for a moment, feeling more annoyed with each passing second. What kind of date was this? She'd be getting the food on her own, then they'd be sitting in a theater for two hours, not talking to each other.

Plus, Livvy had decided she wasn't that hungry for dinner. She wanted to eat hot, buttery popcorn and get a large soda. Since Slade didn't drink soda or eat much junk food, she always felt weird about eating that stuff in front of him.

Ok, she typed back. She was already here, and well, she'd deal with the crowded taco place.

Slade didn't show up until the movie had already started. Livvy ended up buying the tickets, choosing the seats, and then waiting outside the theater holding a greasy fast-food bag like she was some lost soul.

"Hey, Liv," Slade said when he finally arrived. His voice was light and cheerful as if he wasn't forty minutes late.

"Here's your chimichangas." Livvy held out the bag to him.

He took the bag. "Great, thanks! I can't wait to see this movie. I heard it was amazing."

Livvy said nothing, but when he grasped her hand, she softened just a bit.

They found their seats and had only missed some previews. So Livvy decided that things weren't so bad after all. Being the girlfriend of a doctor had its ups and downs. While the last of the previews played, Slade ate his chimichangas, and Livvy regretted not buying popcorn after all.

Just before the lights dimmed for the feature, Mason Rowe walked in. Alone. He carried a giant tub of popcorn and a large drink. He glanced over in Livvy's direction, and the theater went dark seconds later. But she was almost certain he'd seen her.

She couldn't tell how far up the aisle he went above them, but just knowing he was there somewhere in the audience, made her feel guilty all over again.

Mason Rowe had come to the theater by himself.

Or maybe not.

As the opening scene of the western started, Livvy turned to see if she could spot him. But it was too hard to make out faces in the unpredictable light. And so what if he was with someone? In fact, she hoped he was. Then she wouldn't have to feel guilty.

Slade finished with his chimichanga, and Livvy offered to take the sack to the trash.

"Are you sure?" Slade whispered.

"Yeah," Livvy said. "I need to get a quick drink from the water fountain anyway." She rose and crossed the theater, taking glances where she could, scanning for Mason. But she didn't see him.

She returned to Slade, and he linked their hands together. Livvy waited for the swoony feeling, the comfortable, safe feeling, the bonding . . . but her mind wasn't on how it felt to hold hands with Slade. Her mind was on the man she couldn't see.

Ten

Mason knew better than to flatter himself that Livvy was looking for him. He'd watched her turn around several times as if she was trying to find someone behind her. His seat was near the top of the theater on the far right.

Yet . . .

He leaned back and tried to stretch out his legs, but his height made it impossible to get comfortable in a theater chair. At least the movie should be good. The trailer had been interesting, but fifteen minutes into the movie Mason found that he wasn't following the plotline at all. He was watching Livvy and Slade more than he was the screen.

At one point, Slade got up and left, then came back about five minutes later. He didn't sit again though—instead he leaned down and said something to Livvy, then left again.

The hollowness in Mason's gut told him that Slade had just ditched his date.

Mason watched Livvy. She hadn't gone after Slade but

seemed to be watching the movie. When she wiped at her eyes, Mason bit back a curse. She was crying.

He didn't know what possessed him to stand, but before he could reason with himself, he was heading down the aisle. He slid into the seat next to Livvy, and he felt her surprised gaze on him. He didn't look at her though, didn't speak, only handed over the wad of napkins he'd gotten for the popcorn.

She hesitated, then took the napkins. She dabbed at her tears, then whispered, "Thank you."

Mason nodded and set the popcorn between the two of them.

This time, Livvy didn't hesitate. She scooped out a handful of popcorn and started to eat. Mason held back a satisfied smile as he took his own handful.

When he offered over his soda a couple of minutes later, she shook her head no.

"I don't have cooties," he whispered, finally turning to look at her. "And I promise I'm not sick."

The edges of her mouth curved, and she leaned forward and took a sip of the drink while he still held it. Then she sat back in her chair. They continued to watch the movie and eat the popcorn, and Livvy even drank more of the soda.

About halfway through the movie, Livvy leaned over, her shoulder brushing his, and said, "I think I'm lost. What's going on?"

"I'm lost too," Mason said. "I haven't been paying attention."

Livvy laughed, then covered up her mouth.

"Keep it down," Mason whispered in mock seriousness. "I'm trying to watch a movie."

Livvy only laughed more. She leaned forward, stifling her laughter with both hands. Thankfully the musical score of the movie reached a crescendo so her laughter was drowned out.

By the time the movie quieted, Livvy was breathing normally and sitting back in her chair.

Mason had to work hard to keep a straight face. He tried to focus on the dialog and action, but he was way too far behind in the plot to appreciate anything that was going on. He glanced at Livvy to find she was watching the movie intently.

Well, he could keep eating. He reached for more popcorn only to discover they'd eaten the whole tub. "Do you want more popcorn?" he whispered.

She moved her hand to her stomach. "No. I can't eat anymore, or at least I shouldn't."

He set the empty tub on the floor by their feet. When he leaned back again, his arm brushed with hers. She didn't move her arm away, so neither did he.

They watched the rest of the movie that way. Barely touching—yet Mason was aware of every movement, each tiny sound, each breath she took.

When the credits finally rolled, Mason was glad the movie was over, but he also didn't want to say goodbye to Livvy.

Around them, people got to their feet and shuffled out. Livvy didn't make any move to leave, so neither did Mason. He wasn't sure if he'd ever stayed to watch every last scrolling credit before, but it was interesting how many hundreds of names were listed with their particular jobs.

By the time the film shut off, the theater was completely empty.

"So what did you think?" Mason asked.

"Best movie ever?" Livvy quipped.

Mason chuckled. "Agreed. Although I'm not too picky."

Livvy shifted in her seat and faced him. "Thanks for the popcorn and the drink."

"If I knew you were going to eat so much of it, I would have gotten you your own tub," Mason said.

Livvy scoffed and shoved his shoulder. "It was more than half gone when I got my first handful."

"Hold still," he said. Livvy had a tiny crumb of popcorn on her chin, and he brushed it off with his thumb.

She seemed to freeze at his touch.

"Sorry, did you want it left there?" he asked.

Her expression relaxed. "No." Suddenly she rose to her feet. "Thanks for sitting next to me, Mason." Her voice was higher-pitched, faster.

Why was she nervous all of a sudden?

He grabbed the popcorn tub and empty drink cup and stood. "I'm glad you saved a seat for me."

Livvy smirked, but her eyes were too bright. "Yeah, um, Slade was called to the hospital. Sometimes his patients specifically request him. Small town and all."

Mason rocked back on his heels. "I get it. Stuff happens. How are you getting home?"

"Oh, we drove separately."

Mason tried not to look surprised, but he probably failed.

"It was easier for Slade to meet me here," she rushed to say, as if she had to explain. "His schedule's crazy, you know, and well, I didn't mind."

The flush of her face told Mason that she did mind. Besides, she'd used his napkins to dry her tears.

"It's below freezing out there, so the roads are terrible," Mason said. "I can take you home in my Jeep—four-wheel drive and all."

"No, that's okay." Livvy stepped away from him. "My Honda's great in the snow. Not deep snow, but icy roads are fine. I'll take it slow."

Mason exhaled. "I'll follow you then. Make sure you get home okay."

Livvy drew her brows together.

Mason moved past her and tossed his trash into the bin against the wall.

When he turned back to face her, she said, "You don't have to follow me. I'm sure you have other things to do."

"Not really." He shrugged. "The plan of popcorn and a movie was as far as I got."

"Your celebration for writing twenty pages today?" Livvy gave him a knowing smile.

"Yeah, kind of pathetic, huh?"

"Not pathetic." Livvy walked toward him. "I mean, I'm the one who got ditched at a movie. So it's me who's pathetic since I keep thinking that my dates with Slade will have a different outcome."

Mason slipped his hands into his pockets because it reminded him not to touch her. They walked toward the parking lot exit together. Either everyone had already gone to their cars or it was between movies, because the hallway was deserted.

"Do you know what the definition of insanity is?" Mason asked.

Livvy looked up at him, her gaze confused. "Um . . . no . . ."

"It's doing the same thing over and over, and expecting different results." He popped open the exit door, and the chilly wind gusted into the building. He shivered. "How long is winter in Pine Valley?"

"Ha. We're just getting started," she said. "Wait until the middle of January—if you stay that long—then you'll know misery." She pushed the blowing hair from her eyes as they walked to her car. When they reached it, she stopped. "I must be insane."

"To live here?" Mason asked.

"No." She shook her head. "I must be insane to expect Slade to ever make more time for me."

Mason really had no reply to that. Or if he did, it wouldn't be nice. "Get in and warm the car up. I'll clear it off."

He knew she was going to protest, so when she opened her mouth, he said, "Help a guy out who's trying to keep chivalry alive."

Livvy smiled despite the freezing wind, and Mason smiled back.

"All right." She unlocked her car with hands trembling from cold, then started the engine.

Mason set to work, clearing off the snow from the windows and hood of her car with the sleeve of his coat. Then he did a pass over the headlights. He cracked her door open. "Give me a minute to get my Jeep so I can follow. And no speeding, ma'am."

Livvy laughed. "Right."

Mason shut her door, then he jogged to where he'd parked. A couple of minutes later, he pulled his Jeep to where Livvy was waiting to drive away.

The drive to her place took only about twenty minutes, and she pulled up to an older house in a quaint neighborhood. She must have pushed the garage door opener, because the garage started to lift and a light came on. There was another small car parked on the right side of the double garage, and it made Mason feel better to see that her roommate must be home.

He didn't really like the thought of Livvy going home to an empty house after getting ditched by her boyfriend.

He was about to pull away when Livvy came toward him,

walking through all the snow in her unshoveled driveway. He rolled the passenger window down. "Are you locked out or something?"

"No," she said as she reached his Jeep. She rested her forearms on the edge of the door. "Thanks, Mason. I had fun eating your popcorn and watching the movie with you— although I still don't know what happened."

Mason gave her a half-smile. "Any time."

"Tomorrow I'm buying you breakfast," she said.

Mason pictured her showing up at the library with a sack of bagels or muffins, so she completely surprised him when she said, "Do you want to meet at the Main Street Café at 8:00 a.m.? I have the morning shift again, so I have to open the library."

Mason thought of a bunch of questions to ask her— mostly about what would her boyfriend think, and did she really want to be seen with him at her small-town bakery? But he asked none of them. Instead he said, "I'll be there. Now get into your house before you freeze."

Livvy laughed and stepped away from the Jeep. Her laughter was the best thing he'd heard all night. She waved him off, and he pressed on the gas. It was turning out to be a better day than he'd expected. Maybe tomorrow he'd write another twenty pages.

Eleven

$\mathcal{L}$ ivvy slept like a rock, and so when her alarm went off, it took her a moment to orient herself. She grappled for her cell phone and pushed STOP on the alarm. She wondered why she'd set her alarm so early, then she remembered. She'd invited Mason to breakfast.

Last night it had seemed like the right thing to do—the best thing—and it was what she wanted to do. This morning . . . she knew she'd gotten herself into hot water. Could she cancel? Come up with some kind of excuse?

No, she didn't have his phone number. Besides, *she* wasn't Slade. She wasn't going to cancel on Mason.

They were officially friends now; well, they had been for weeks. And she could meet him for breakfast without any other motive or agenda. If Slade found out, then he found out. Or maybe she'd outright tell him just in case some busybody spotted them at the café and decided to report back to Slade. Well, she'd just own it. Sarah Lynne was probably working there, and she was someone whom Livvy didn't have to worry about gossiping.

Livvy climbed out of bed and took a quick shower, then she dressed in her black jeans and white-and-black sweater. She pulled on her boots, which had dried overnight. Then she twisted her hair into a clip.

A snowplow rumbled past the house, and Livvy went into the living room to look out the window. Apparently it had stopped snowing, but the sky seemed to promise more. And it was seven forty-five, time for Livvy to start driving. She hoped that Mallory wouldn't be too mad at her for leaving and not shoveling.

The drive to the café took twenty minutes. Everyone was driving slow, which was good, but Livvy hated to think of Mason at the café wondering if she was really going to show up.

When she walked in, the heat of the café was warm and cozy, and the scent of baking muffins, cinnamon rolls, and coffee was divine. A man sat in the corner, but she didn't see Mason.

"Hi, Sarah," she said to the woman at the counter.

"I haven't seen you in a while," Sarah Lynne said. Her blonde hair was pulled into its usual smooth ponytail.

"Yeah, the library has been keeping me busy," Livvy said. "We put in a new inventory system last month, and we're still catching up."

"Sounds fun," Sarah teased as she opened the display case. "Want to try some samples?"

"Uh, I'm . . . meeting someone." Livvy turned to look toward the entrance, then she did a double take when she focused on the man in the corner. The man *was* Mason, and he'd . . . shaved his beard.

He unfolded himself from his chair. "Glad you made the drive okay."

She stared at him, saying nothing. Livvy could admit she'd grown used to his beard, and that he was a good-looking man with it. Besides, it sort of went with his whole lumberjack persona. His thick plaid shirts, jeans, and heavy boots. But now . . . "What happened to you?"

His brows shot up, and his baby blues twinkled. "What are you talking about?"

"You know." She waved her hand as she walked toward him. "Your beard. It's gone."

Mason ran his hand over his chin. "Now you miss it?"

Her face heated, and she glanced over at Sarah. Sarah kept her gaze averted, solely focusing on stirring something on the back counter. "I—I don't miss it," Livvy said in a low voice. "I mean . . . did you shave it because of what I said?"

His mouth quirked. "I thought it was time for a new look."

She rested her hands on her hips. "I didn't expect you to shave," she said. "I mean, you looked fine with it."

"Now you tell me."

Livvy's mouth fell open. "You *did* shave for me."

He didn't reply, just kept those blue eyes focused on hers. She stepped forward, and against her better judgement, she reached up and ran her fingers over his smooth jaw. "Did it take a long time?"

"Not that long," he said.

She felt the vibrations of his voice against her fingertips, and she suddenly became very aware that she was touching his face in a public café, even though Sarah was the only other one in the shop.

Livvy dropped her hand and ignored the butterflies that had erupted inside of her.

"If it's any consolation, I didn't recognize him at first either," Sarah said from behind the counter.

So she had been listening in. Livvy knew her face was red. "You know each other?" she said in a friendly tone, turning to face Sarah.

Sarah's smile was casual. "Well, he has been coming here for breakfast every morning for the past several weeks."

Livvy hated that she felt jealous. It was ridiculous to feel that way. Sarah was a pretty woman, divorced with a two-year-old son. She was probably in the dating scene again. And it wasn't like Livvy owned Mason or anything. She had a boy-friend, for heaven's sake.

She looked back to Mason and found that his gaze was on *her*, not Sarah. The tightening in Livvy's stomach eased a touch. "Hungry?"

"Starving."

Again. Butterflies. "Great." Livvy walked to the counter, Mason beside her. "I'll get the egg croissant and the hot cocoa with extra whipped cream. And then whatever he wants. I'm paying."

She could hear a smile in Mason's voice when he said, "I'll get the same thing."

Sarah nodded. "Two egg croissants and hot cocoas coming up." She turned away to start preparing the food.

Livvy and Mason walked back to the table in the corner, closest to the window that overlooked Main Street. The traffic was starting to build up, and Livvy noticed that most of the shops had already decorated for Christmas although it wasn't even Thanksgiving.

Livvy folded her hands on top of the table to keep from fidgeting. Her gaze strayed to the window, mostly so that she wouldn't keep staring at Mason's clean-shaven face.

She was sure there would be plenty of customers who'd come into the café and see her with Mason. So she wanted to mentally prepare herself to tell Slade before he heard it from someone else. As if on cue, the door jangled, and two people walked in. It was an older couple that Livvy had seen about town over the past year. She didn't recall their names, so she just nodded.

"So what do you usually order here?" Livvy asked, glancing at Mason.

He leaned forward and rested his forearms on the table. "Coffee and bagels. Sometimes a muffin. Haven't tried the egg croissant before."

"Then you're in for a treat," she said.

He nodded. "I cook eggs for dinner—some sort of omelet. I don't have very refined cooking skills."

"I'm not much of a cook either," she said. "My roommate, Mallory, will make main dishes, and I've become pretty adept at the side dishes."

Sarah appeared then, bringing their food and drinks.

Livvy tamped down the unreasonable envy she felt when Sarah smiled at Mason as he thanked her. Livvy had Mr. Dreamy Doc. Why should she be critical of Sarah or Mason, or the fact that Mason saw Sarah every morning? He had to eat somewhere.

While Livvy was wrapped up in her swirling thoughts, Mason started eating the egg croissant. "Mm. This is good."

Focus, Livvy. "Glad you like it." She took her own bite, then sipped the hot cocoa. It was a little too hot still, and she reached for the water glass that Sarah had also thoughtfully delivered.

"I haven't had cocoa in a long time," Mason said. "My mom used to make it when I was a kid."

Livvy liked that Mason was talking about himself without

being prompted. She wondered if he took after his dad or his mom. "Are your parents still in Colorado?"

"Sort of," he said. He used a napkin to wipe his mouth, and Livvy looked away from his lips. "They've both passed away, but they're buried in my hometown."

Oh. "Oh, I'm sorry," Livvy said. She was at loss for what else to say.

Mason didn't seem to mind the intrusion though. "My mom got breast cancer when I was a teenager. She had a phobia of doctors and hospitals, so she didn't get diagnosed until she was stage four."

"I had no idea," Livvy said in a quiet voice. She thought of her vibrant mother, who was still running half-marathons; Livvy had never really caught the running bug. Mason's mother must have been quite young when she died.

"My dad was never the same," Mason continued. "He was the high school basketball coach where I played and went to school, and we were already at odds with each other most of the time. Our relationship only deteriorated after my mom died. A few years ago, he had a massive heart attack."

Livvy covered her mouth.

"I can't say I was surprised that he died that way," Mason said in a matter-of-fact tone. "He lived with a lot of anger for a long time. It finally caught up with him."

"What was he angry about?" She lowered her hand. "Your mother's death?"

"He was angry he didn't make her see the doctor sooner," Mason said. "He was angry when she refused chemotherapy. He was angry when I fouled out in games, and when I did it during the state championship, he never let go of his grudge. He was angry when I accepted an athletic scholarship to play basketball out of state. He hated traveling, you see. His back hurt too much to make a long drive and he hated flying. Claustrophobic."

"Did he ever come to your games?" she asked in a hesitant tone.

"Two games, ones that were played in neighboring states." Mason shrugged. "Then I blew my knee out."

He might have been acting nonchalant, and several years might have passed, but the pain was still evident in his eyes. Livvy wondered who'd helped him through the deaths of each of his parents?

"Hey there," a man said behind Livvy, interrupting the somber spell that had settled over their table.

Livvy turned to see Dawson Harris. "Hi, Dawson." She ran into him once in a while, and when she'd first moved here, she once thought he was going to ask her out. But he never did, and Livvy had no regrets. She wasn't really into lawyer types. Especially now that she knew what he'd said to Mason about staying away from her, courtesy of Slade.

Dawson grinned as if he was happier than a Cheshire cat seeing her sitting with Mason. "Nice to see you again, Mason."

"Is it?" Mason said, his smile equally brassy.

Livvy wanted to kick both men. "Any big court cases today, Dawson?" she said to diffuse the situation.

Dawson lifted one of his eyebrows. "Not until two. Grabbing a bite to eat before some client meetings."

"Well, good luck this afternoon," Livvy said, pointedly dismissing him.

"Thanks, I appreciate it." Dawson nodded to Mason, then continued on his way to order at the counter.

"If he sits near us, I'm leaving," Livvy said under her breath.

Mason's brows popped up. "You really don't like him?"

"I don't like what he said to you in the gym the other day."

This time, Mason's smile was genuine. "You're defending *me?*"

Twelve

Mason had pretty much spilled his long, sad tale over breakfast, and then Livvy started acting as skittish as a hare during hunting season. She hadn't even finished the food she'd claimed to love so much, and Mason figured that had a lot to do with Dawson Harris's appearance.

The hardening knot in Mason's stomach told him that Livvy hadn't wanted to be spotted out in public with him. Yet she'd invited *him* and had chosen the place. Now his mind wouldn't focus on his writing, and he was beyond frustrated. It was almost noon, and he'd written nothing.

He couldn't see the reference desk from his position, and so he stood and walked until he spotted Livvy working on a computer. He hesitated, not wanting to disturb her, but also knowing that they needed to talk about a few things before he could focus on writing again.

Only a couple of tables were occupied, and no one seemed to be paying attention to Mason. So he made his way to the reference counter.

Livvy lifted her head as he approached. Something like guilt filled her expression, and she clicked her mouse a few times before turning to face him.

"Hey," Mason said.

Lines appeared between her brows. "How do you do it all?"

This wasn't what Mason had expected her to say. "What do you mean?"

Livvy bit her lip, and Mason tried not to notice the berry color. Her usually pale pink lips were now darker and shinier. She must be wearing lip gloss.

"Your parents are both gone," she said, "and you went through a serious injury in college, and then the lawsuit last year—"

"Whoa, whoa," Mason said, holding up his hand. "Life's hard for everyone. I hope you don't think I was dumping on you at breakfast."

"No, not at all." Livvy pushed away from the reference counter and came around to stand by him. "I'm only wondering who, besides your agent, supports you."

Mason shrugged. "My editor is pretty nice—most of the time. And I have a couple of writing buddies I see once or twice a year at events."

Livvy kept staring at him, and Mason was beginning to feel too warm.

"You're missing the beard, aren't you?" he teased. He wanted to see the happy Livvy, not the serious one looking at him.

"Mason," she said, then took a deep breath. She grasped his arm and tugged him forward.

Surprised, he moved with her until she stopped in one of the book aisles, out of sight from anyone who might come into the library. She released his arm and rested her hands on her hips.

"I think I know why you got writer's block," she said in a low voice. "I mean, you've gone through a lot, and you've dealt with it all on your own, until it became too much. The lawsuit was like the tipping scale."

He had no idea where she was going with this, but standing so close together in a secluded aisle of books was probably not the best idea. She smelled like cinnamon and vanilla and something sweeter. Berries. Was it the lip gloss?

"Most people have someone to talk to when they're going through a hard time," she continued.

"Believe me, my agent and publisher and two lawyers were always having conference calls," Mason said. She was definitely wearing lip gloss. "They talked so much, I started getting headaches."

But Livvy wasn't deterred. "I meant talking to someone who cares about *you,* beyond your career. Someone who doesn't have a monetary interest or financial investment."

"Like a shrink?"

Livvy swatted his arm and scoffed. "No. Like a girlfriend, or a wife, or a friend you can confide in."

"And . . . your point?"

She folded her arms. "My point is that once you started coming to the library and spent time around regular people, even if you weren't talking to them, you could suddenly write." A smile touched the edges of her berry lips. "You need people, Mason."

An interesting theory, he decided, though one that he could probably argue with.

She lifted her hand and pressed a finger against his chest. "I'm going to organize a small get-together. I'll invite my best friends, and you can get to know more people in Pine Valley.

Who knows, maybe you'll like my friends and they'll become *your* friends, too."

Mason exhaled. He leaned toward her a few inches and placed a hand on the bookcase shelf behind her. "I don't think so."

More lines appeared between her brows, but she didn't move away from his nearness. "You won't even consider it?"

"I have that deadline I told you about, remember?" Mason scanned her face, from her brown eyes to her berry lips to the freckle just above her mouth. "And why would I spend time with other people when I already know that I'd prefer to hang out with *one* person?"

She blinked.

"Did you know you have a freckle above your lip?" he said in a low voice.

She raised her chin slightly, and he lifted his hand at the same time. With one finger he touched her freckle.

"My mom used to tell me it was an angel kiss," she whispered against his finger.

The edges of her clothing brushed against the edges of his, creating a dangerous heat between them. His breathing went shallow, matching hers, and his pulse drummed hard. It would be so easy to kiss her right now, and he didn't think she'd complain. But she had a boyfriend. And unless she called things off with Slade—

Livvy grasped the collar of his shirt and pulled him toward her. And then her mouth was on his, or his was on hers. It was hard to know who'd started kissing whom first. All Mason knew was that her mouth was sweet and warm and she tasted of sugar and cinnamon and everything he couldn't have.

Mason kept one hand gripping the bookshelf as he deepened the kiss. He moved his other hand behind her neck, tangling his fingers into her curls. Her hair was soft, and she seemed to melt against him as they kissed. Livvy released his collar, then trailed her hands down his chest, making him shudder at her touch.

He felt her smile against his mouth. She was being a little vixen, and as if to prove that point, she slid her hands around his torso, anchoring him against her.

"Livvy," he whispered, trying to make sense of the rising passion between them. "We shouldn't be—"

"No talking in the library," she whispered, cutting off all protest.

He chuckled and let go of the bookshelf, then skimmed his hand down her back. Their kissing slowed, but the heat only built, and Livvy didn't seem to be letting go any time soon. Mason certainly wasn't going to stop her, but he was also aware that they were kissing in the library, with only a shelf of books separating them from anyone who might walk by. Plus Livvy was off limits. Yet who was he to remind her?

The heat of her mouth, the softness of her curves, the tug of her hands on his clothing to drag him closer, all swirled together in his mind until everything else was forgotten. The snow. The boyfriend. The lawsuit. The deadline.

In this space, and in this moment, only he and Livvy existed.

He moved his hand along the curve of her waist as he kissed her warm mouth, then he settled both hands on her hips, noting how perfectly she fit against him.

She sighed. "Mason."

"What?" he murmured.

"Nothing," she whispered.

And then they were kissing again. Mason rotated so that his back was against the shelves. She rose up on her toes, making her face more level with his. He sensed her returning to earth as she drew away and met his gaze.

"Livvy . . ." he tried again.

But she shook her head, wrapped her arms about his neck, then nestled her face against his skin. Her warm breath tickled his neck, and he broke out in goose bumps.

He closed his eyes and ran his hand up her back, over her shoulders, skimming her neck, then slid his thumb along the soft skin of her jaw.

"Please don't throw any parties." He felt her smile against his skin. "You're all the distraction I can take."

"What about Thanksgiving?" she whispered.

"I don't like turkey."

She drew away from him then, not too far though, so that she was still in his arms. "You're kidding."

He kissed the edge of her jaw. "I'm not kidding."

"What do you usually do for Thanksgiving?" she asked, her eyes fluttering shut as he kissed the edge of her mouth.

"Write, watch football, bake frozen pizza. Write some more."

Her lips curved upward, and he kissed her freckle.

"You're a nut," she said with a laugh.

"Probably." He kissed her lips this time. She didn't hesitate to kiss him back, and he wondered if he'd ever become so lost in a woman before.

The sound of voices came from the direction of the reference desk, and it was clear that someone was asking where the librarian was.

Livvy drew away, although she didn't release him. Her cheeks were flushed, her lips rosy, and her eyes smiling. "I think I'd better go."

"Do you want me to wait here for you?"

She stifled a laugh. "Uh, I should get back to work, and you should too."

Mason slid his hands down her arms and linked their fingers. "I'm going to the gym for a couple of hours."

"What are you doing tonight?" she asked.

"Depends on you," he said.

She released one of his hands and pulled her cell phone from her pocket. "Put your number in my phone. I'll be right back."

He took the phone, then kissed her forehead before he completely released her.

After she left, he pulled up her contacts and added his name and number, then the address of his cabin, even though she knew where it was. His heart was still racing, and he didn't want to analyze what had just happened between them. Or wonder what it had meant— *to her*—or to him.

She was still at the reference desk when his head started to clear. Things were getting complicated in Pine Valley. He'd spent the morning either thinking about Livvy or kissing her, and now he had nothing written. He hoped that a long run in the gym might put him back into the frame of mind to write this afternoon.

He walked through the library, gathered up his things, then set Livvy's cell phone on the reference counter while she was still talking to an older couple about something to do with the history of Pine Valley. She glanced up at him, an adorable blush coloring her face, and he winked, then strode out of the building.

The cold wind bit into his skin, blowing away all the warmth he'd sustained from Livvy.

As he made his way through the parking lot, the complication of being in a relationship with a woman like Livvy began to force itself to his cognizance. Her boyfriend was the first hurdle. How serious were they? And what about the fact that Mason lived in San Diego? Not to mention, he could feel himself becoming distracted from his book. He'd had three great weeks, and now he was putting that in jeopardy.

He unlocked his Jeep and climbed into the cold interior. Starting the engine, he turned up the heat full blast. Had Livvy been right? Did he need more human interaction? Was that why writing in the library had been what broke through his block? Could he do both . . . be with Livvy and get his manuscript done?

Mason groaned as he steered onto the main road. Kissing Livvy had been amazing. *She* was amazing. Beautiful, witty, soft, sexy. Too tempting. And despite his resolve to not overanalyze their kiss in the library—well, kissing *session*—he wondered what it had meant to her . . . She was the one who had the boyfriend. Would she tell Slade? Would she brush off Mason?

Would she play both sides?

No, Mason decided. She wasn't the type.

What type was she? She was a nice girl, the girl-next-door type, who trusted people. Gave them lots of chances. She didn't even curse. Mason groaned again. What had he done? He had no place in her life. She was settled in Pine Valley, ran the gorgeous library, and dated the most eligible bachelor in town—and . . . Mason was a fly-by-night.

He already knew *he* wasn't *her* type. He'd been alone since his mother had died, which seemed so long ago that he couldn't remember what it felt like to have any type of love in his life. Not that he was in love with Livvy or thought he would fall in love with her.

Maybe if the circumstances were completely different.

Maybe if he'd met her in San Diego. And she was the librarian there and didn't have a doctor boyfriend. Maybe . . . maybe . . . maybe . . .

Thirteen

*L*ivvy might have knocked a little too aggressively on Felicity's door, because when she answered it, her green eyes were like giant saucers behind her turquoise-rimmed glasses.

"You okay?" Felicity asked.

"No," Livvy declared, moving past her friend and into the living room. She sank onto the couch and pulled her knees up to her chest. "*I kissed him.* I mean it was more of a make out. And it was amazing . . ." She groaned and buried her face in her hands. She felt the cushion shift next to her.

Felicity grasped her shoulder. "Wait. That's a good thing, right? You finally broke the ice with Slade—so what if you had to instigate it? He probably didn't mind in the least—"

Livvy raised her head and stared at her friend. "You don't understand," she said in a choked voice. "I kissed *Mason.*"

Felicity's eyebrows popped up. "Mason? *The writer?* Lumberjack man? Mr. Dark & Broody?"

"Stop," Livvy choked out. "And yes, I kissed Mason Rowe. A lot. In the library."

Felicity opened her mouth, but nothing came out.

"I know." Livvy sighed. "I have no words either. I practically jumped him, and then he even tried to warn me, but I was like a crazy woman. He was just so . . . And I was . . . He shaved his beard, did I tell you? He shaved it for me. And those blue eyes of his seem to always look right into my soul, and it was like I couldn't *not* kiss him. You know?"

Felicity was still staring at her, saying nothing. And then her mouth quirked.

"You are not going to laugh at me."

Felicity turned away, covering her mouth.

"It's not funny," Livvy said. "He's working on a deadline—for a major book that will probably be a *New York Times* bestseller—and I just accosted him in a book aisle."

Felicity was laughing now, there was no denying it.

Livvy leaned her head back on the couch and closed her eyes. "What am I going to tell Slade?"

Felicity stopped laughing.

Livvy didn't dare open her eyes to see the expression on Felicity's face now. Livvy's stomach hadn't stopped flipping since, well, since this morning when Mason had told her about his family. She didn't know why she'd thought kissing him would be a good idea in any universe.

Perhaps the beard had been the thing to keep her from grabbing his shirt collar and pulling him toward her the day before, or the day before that . . . But had that been all it took? Mason to shave his beard? No . . . Mason was attractive, kind, funny, broody—yes, smart . . .

But she'd dated Slade four months before they'd kissed, and he was her dream man. Her doctor. And she'd never made a move first, until Mason.

She groaned. "Mason must think I'm a two-timer and a total floozy. I asked him to breakfast, and I paid, so that was kind of like a date. It was like my psyche was planning to attack him without my brain knowing about it."

Felicity still wasn't talking.

Livvy opened her eyes to see that Felicity was leaning back on the couch too, staring at her in wonder.

"Say something, please," Livvy said. "Tell me that I'm dreaming. That I didn't just have the best kiss of my life with a man who is *not* a doctor."

Felicity smiled.

"Don't laugh."

"I'm not," Felicity said, although she sounded on the verge of laughing. "I'm sorry that you're so . . . distressed over this, but I'm not surprised."

"What do you mean?" Livvy frowned. "You're not surprised that I attacked poor Mason Rowe in the library, or you're not surprised that doctors aren't better kissers?"

Felicity pulled her feet up and sat cross-legged while facing Livvy. "I hate to break it to you, but Slade is kind of a jerk when it comes to relationships. So I don't blame you for kissing the man you see every day and the man who actually listens to you and wants to spend time with you."

"Does this mean I'm desperate for affection or something?" Livvy asked.

"I don't know what it means," Felicity said, all laughter gone from her tone now. "Although, you were the one who built up an entire fantasy relationship with a doctor *before* you even met Slade. So I think reality is calling BS on your boyfriend fantasies."

Livvy bit her lip. Which kind of still felt bruised from all that kissing. Mason might have tried to stop her a time or two, but he'd kept up his end of the kissing match quite well. A warm shiver went through her at the thought of his hands on her, his mouth on hers, his smile, his whispered words . . .

"Liv?" Felicity prompted.

"Okay, here's the thing," Livvy said, pulling one of the throw pillows and squeezing it against her chest. "I was caught up in the moment. It was a mistake."

"Slade's still the one?" Felicity said.

"Of course." Livvy held out her phone to Felicity, and she leaned over to read the text that Slade had sent twenty minutes ago.

Hey, Liv. Do you have Thanksgiving plans? If you're not going to your parents, do you want to come to mine?

Felicity brought a hand to her mouth to cover up a gasp.

"I know, right?" Livvy put the phone on the coffee table because she didn't want to read the text that should have made her feel like she'd won the lottery. The invitation that she'd been hoping would come—to meet Slade's parents. And on a *family* holiday. In other words, they'd be a *couple*, and she'd be introduced as his girlfriend.

She should be celebrating. She should be jumping up and down and feeling giddy. But all she felt was guilty.

"So . . ." Felicity smoothed back her brunette hair. "If you hadn't kissed Mason today, how would this text make you feel?"

Livvy frowned. "What do you mean? I'm happy about the invitation. It's the next step in my relationship with Slade."

"You don't look happy," Felicity countered. "You look pretty miserable."

"That's because I did a stupid thing, and now I have to tell Slade," Livvy said. "He'll probably dump me. Mason will see right through me. And I'll be going home for Thanksgiving to sulk."

"You don't have to tell Slade," Felicity said. "I doubt Mason is going to be announcing it to anyone."

Livvy worried her lip again. "Good point."

"But . . ."

"But if Slade had kissed another girl, I'd want to know."

Felicity nodded. "Would you break up with him?"

Exhaling, Livvy thought about it. "Probably. Which means that I shouldn't tell Slade if I want to stay together. Which will only bring me more guilt." Livvy buried her face in her hands again, and Felicity rubbed her back.

Livvy couldn't believe she'd gotten herself into this situation. She didn't want to hurt either man. She didn't want to play them off each other. Slade was . . . her dream. Mason was . . . temporary. A diversion? Another fantasy?

She lifted her head. "What if Mason thinks I'm looking for a hookup? That I'm only fangirling."

"Are you?" Felicity asked.

Livvy rubbed her face. "Neither . . . I mean I am a huge fan, but I'm not that type of woman. Or at least, I didn't think I was. My actions have been pretty rotten."

"I'm making hot chocolate," Felicity said, rising from the couch. "Everything will seem better after you've gotten some chocolate in your system."

"I don't think even chocolate can fix this," Livvy said.

"I have ice cream, too."

"Mint chocolate chip?"

"Of course."

Two hours later, Livvy woke up. Apparently she'd fallen asleep on Felicity's couch after her self-induced sugar coma. When the memories of the day came flooding back to Livvy, she had to check her phone to be sure that it wasn't all some horrible dream. Yep, there was Slade's text about Thanksgiving—which she still hadn't answered. And . . . yep, there was Mason Rowe's number saved in her contacts. He'd even added the address of his cabin *and* his San Diego address. *Hmm. Interesting.* She didn't know how much to read into that.

Livvy sat up and ran a hand over her hair. She could hear some music playing, or maybe it was a TV, coming from Felicity's bedroom. Darkness had fallen, and although Livvy only lived a few houses down, she was reluctant to go back home. Her roommate, Mallory, knew little about all that had gone on with Mason, just that he was writing at the library, and it would be hard to keep her current mood hidden.

The fewer people who knew about Livvy's screwup, the better. She scrolled through her texts with Slade. She'd kept their conversations from the very first text, and Livvy remembered how flattered she'd been in the beginning. She was still flattered, and now he'd asked her to a major family event.

Yet the invitation felt like a rock in her stomach. What would happen when she told Slade about kissing another man? Would he dump her on the spot? Would he be angry? Would he forgive her? Would he ever trust her again?

Livvy blew out a breath and rose from the couch, then folded the blanket that Felicity must have draped over her. She walked down the hall to Felicity's bedroom and knocked on the door, then cracked it open.

Felicity was stretched out on her bed, reading a book while music played.

"Hi," Livvy said, hovering in the doorway. "Thanks for the chocolate and the couch and for letting me dump on you."

Felicity sat up on the bed and patted the area next to her. So Livvy walked into the room and sat by her.

"Okay, I need to tell you something that you might not agree with," Felicity said. "But I've been thinking while you've been asleep. I also might have googled 'how to know if a guy likes you' and 'ten ways to save a relationship' and finally 'how to know when a kiss means he's into you.'"

"What?" Livvy said with a laugh. "I kissed *him*, remember."

Felicity smiled. "But he kissed you back, and by your description, it wasn't a quick peck."

Heat rose in Livvy's face. "Not quick at all."

"So . . ." Felicity said, adjusting her glasses, then folding her hands in her lap. "Since I've become quite a relationship expert in the last two hours, I'm advising you not to tell Slade yet."

Livvy blinked. "Why not?"

"You need to find out if Mason is a fling or if you really like him," Felicity said. "If you really like him, then break up with Slade. If Mason is a fling, and you're still devoted to Slade, then beg for Slade's forgiveness."

Livvy bit one of her nails even though she hadn't bitten her nails since she was seven and her mom had painted on that nasty oil. "Sounds . . . tricky. I mean, how am I supposed to know if I really like Mason? And how do I know if he really likes *me?*"

"That's the hard part," Felicity said. "You're going to have to spend more time with him, and you'll probably have to ask him straight out."

Livvy scoffed. "I'm not going to have 'the talk' after a first kiss. It was more flirty than anything, casual . . . a one-time thing."

Felicity arched her brows.

"Okay, so is it horrible to admit that I'm insanely attracted to Mason?" Livvy said in a half-whisper. "He's good-looking, but it's much more than that. We connect, and he seems to always be around. And his brain fascinates me, and—" She cut herself off and slumped.

"You have a week until Thanksgiving," Felicity said. "You'll know by then. Accept Slade's invitation. Figure out how you feel about Mason. It will never be too late to change your dinner plans. You can always come here."

"You're not going home?" Livvy asked.

"I have to work the Black Friday sales," Felicity said. "So I don't want to have to make the trek back and forth in a single day."

Livvy blew out a breath. "Okay, if I don't go to Slade's, then I'll have dinner with you."

Fourteen

Mason didn't really expect Livvy to call him, although she now had his number. But he kept checking his phone. Even when he turned up the ringer, set it on the kitchen counter, then went into the other room to try to write a few pages, he still got up to check the phone.

She wasn't going to call. It was too late now, nearly ten o'clock, and besides, she was probably trying to figure out how to politely tell him to leave her alone. He, of course, would oblige, but he wouldn't be happy about it. Yes, it was the right thing to do. Not only because of the boyfriend situation or the fact his home was in San Diego, but what she'd said to him had made him think. Deeply. And they weren't pleasant thoughts.

He had lived a loveless life for years. His mother had been the only one he'd felt unconditional love from. Sure, his father loved him on the level that he could—a level that pretty much only connected them by biology. And his agent, Jolene? If he stopped writing altogether, their relationship would eventually dissolve to annual holiday cards—from her side. He'd never sent a holiday card in his life, and he wasn't about to start now.

When the lawsuit had blown up in his face, it was true that there hadn't been anyone there for him. The fact hadn't occurred to him, thus it hadn't bothered him one bit. Until now. Was he subhuman or something? No. If he were, he wouldn't be emotionally affected by things like lawsuits, name slandering, and looming deadlines. He'd be able to work without caring about much else. Get his manuscripts turned in, collect royalty checks, pay the bills.

Dammit. He did care. He cared that he'd become such a recluse. He cared that Livvy might right now be wondering how to let him down. He cared about her and her small-town life, and his aching heart proved it.

Mason paced the floors of the cabin, walking from the plush rug to the expensive hardwood to the Italian tile, then back to the rug that muffled his frustrated steps.

He *liked* Livvy.

Sure, she had flaws like any other person. The biggest one by the name of *Slade*. But her complexities were endearing and somewhat adorable. And that kiss in the library . . . was the most authentic and genuine experience he'd ever had. Her desire for him had been palpable, and this was why he couldn't write tonight. Livvy had bewitched him.

She'd crept her way into the corners of his life and blown away the cobwebs.

He needed to speak to her, even if it was to hear the dreaded words. He needed to have closure on what had been building between them for the past weeks. Perhaps they could come to some sort of agreement. She'd stay at her end of the library, and he'd stay at his end. He'd wish her well with the doc and everything else in her life at Pine Valley.

She'd read his book when it finally released next summer and maybe email him through his website. They'd exchange a few emails and reminisce. And this time next year, they'd only be a fond memory in each other's lives.

No.

That's not what Mason wanted at all. But what choice did he have?

His phone rang, and Mason nearly tripped in his hurry to grab it from the kitchen counter.

Jolene.

Mason hesitated before answering, but he knew Jolene would call back in five minutes.

"Hello," he grumped.

"Good evening. I guess we're getting straight to the point, then?" Jolene said, her tone cautious.

Mason sank onto the barstool next to the counter. "A few paragraphs today. Nothing substantial." He felt Jolene's disappointment all the way from New York.

"Did you do anything different today?" she asked.

Mason laughed. It wasn't a warm laugh.

She waited.

Mason knew he couldn't hide things from his agent, at least not things that slowed his progress. "I might have gotten a little too caught up in the quaint things of Pine Valley."

"Is one of those things named Olivia Harmon?" Jolene asked, her tone exasperated.

"Livvy," he corrected.

Jolene sighed. Then she changed tactics. "A day of no writing isn't too much to stress over. Get some sleep. Start fresh tomorrow."

"I will," Mason said. "I want to establish a new routine anyway. I can't always write at a library."

"No, you can't," Jolene said in a firm voice. "I'll look forward to speaking tomorrow night."

"See you." Mason hung up. The quiet cabin felt hollow. Empty like his heart and his life. He needed to forget today.

He had no alcohol in the cabin, which was probably a good thing. So he'd sit in the hot tub until he felt relaxed enough to sleep. Since he hadn't brought a swimsuit, he changed into his gym shorts and grabbed a towel. The hot tub was always kept warm, and it didn't take too long for the heater to make it steamy.

Mason stepped into the water, sat down, then leaned his head back and closed his eyes, trying to let his mind go numb. The heated water and the bubbles were soothing. Maybe he should do this every night.

He was somewhere between half-awake and half-asleep when his phone rang. He snapped his head up and eyed his phone where he'd set it atop the towel. Would Jolene call him back so soon? He groaned and moved across the hot tub to look at the phone.

Livvy.

Mason patted one hand on the towel in an effort to dry it, then he picked up the cell and answered, hoping that he didn't sound half-asleep.

"Where are you?" Livvy asked.

This stopped his muddled thoughts. "Are you at the cabin?"

"I am."

Goose bumps skittered along Mason's body. "I'm in the hot tub. Hang on, I'll get out and open the door."

"No, that's okay," she said. "I'll come around back. I don't want to be a bother."

Before he could protest, she'd hung up.

Mason debated whether he should get out and wrap up in the towel, or if . . . maybe he could entice her to join him. He liked the second idea better.

So he settled back into his place, and moments later, Livvy appeared near the stone wall. Her white coat—the same one he knew wasn't all that warm—glowed beneath the moonlight.

She climbed over the wall, then landed on the other side.

"Where are your boots?" Mason asked as she neared. "Your feet are going to freeze. Again."

Livvy laughed, and the sound wrapped its way around his heart. She reached the deck and stamped the snow from her shoes. "You and your obsession with my feet."

Mason grinned. "You wore tennis shoes? Good choice."

"I wasn't planning on hiking through two feet of snow."

"I could have opened the front door," he said.

Livvy shook her head. "I don't want to bother you more than I already have. I just needed to talk to you for a minute."

Mason's stomach went hollow.

"At least put your feet in," he said, trying to keep his tone light. "You can use my towel to dry them after."

Livvy walked to the edge of the hot tub and peered into the water.

The glow from the hot tub lights in combination with her white coat made her skin look ethereal. Which she pretty much was. The woman of an unattainable dream.

"All right." Livvy sat on the edge by the steps, opposite from Mason. She slipped off her tennis shoes, then peeled off her socks.

"Are those Wonder Woman socks?" Mason asked, holding back a laugh. "I don't suppose those come in wool?"

Livvy smirked. "They don't come in wool, but they're

perfectly warm when I'm walking on dry pavement." She tugged the hem of her jeans above each calf.

"I don't think there's going to be dry pavement in Pine Valley for quite a while," he said.

Livvy only smiled as she dipped her feet into the water and set them on the top step.

"Are you sure you don't want to come all the way in?" Mason said. "You could strip down, and I won't look."

Livvy's brows rose.

"To your underwear, of course," he said. "You know, like a bikini."

"I don't think that would be a good idea," Livvy said, her tone serious.

Mason reached for the switch that controlled the jets and turned it off. The sound of the hot tub diminished, and as the quiet settled, he said, "I guess we do need to talk."

Livvy nodded, and he wished he could read her expression.

"I don't know what came over me earlier today in the library," she said in a soft voice, looking down at the water. "So I came to apologize. It wasn't fair of me to, uh, approach you like that, and I'm sorry. It shouldn't have happened."

"It's been a strange couple of days," Mason said. "But don't worry, I'm not offended."

Livvy sighed and shed her coat. Then she leaned forward and skimmed her fingers over the water. "I've never been impulsive like that, and I don't want you to think I regularly accost men. I mean . . . we've been friends, and I hate to ruin that."

Mason smiled. "We're still friends. And I probably shouldn't admit this, but I've been thinking about kissing you for a while now, though I considered you off limits."

Her gaze connected with his. "You've thought . . . about kissing me?"

Mason raised his arms and rested them on the wall behind him so that he could cut down on the heat coursing through him. "Yeah."

Livvy's cheeks flushed pink. "For . . . how long?"

Mason shrugged a shoulder. "Since the lodge."

"The *lodge?*" she asked. "You mean when you gave me the rice bag?"

Mason could only nod.

"But . . . we'd just barely met, and I was a brat."

"I was attracted to you, and it crossed my mind," Mason said. "It wasn't like I was going to act upon it though, especially when you informed me about your doctor boyfriend."

She seemed to cringe, and Mason was pleased to see it. When she didn't say anything, he continued, because he really had nothing to lose at this point. "I'm attracted to you, Livvy. And I like you. It's a fact. But I'm only in Pine Valley until my book's finished, and then I'll be heading back home."

"I know." Her voice was small.

"So maybe you're just a distraction to my work," he said. "Or I'm a distraction to your frustrations with your boyfriend, and things happened between us. No hard feelings on my part."

She exhaled and looked down at the water again. He expected her to agree, and then they could talk about how they'd still be friends. She'd put her shoes back on, and he'd see her in brief moments at the library. They'd share a short hello, a fleeting smile. Nothing more.

But she wasn't responding; she wasn't agreeing with his assessment.

"Or . . . maybe we're *not* distractions to each other."

Mason rose to his feet, and the water rippled around him as he walked toward her.

She watched him approach, her eyes widening. But her gaze wasn't wary, in fact, it was welcoming.

Mason stopped in front of her, and the water swirled about his waist and her calves. "Maybe there is something real between us, and we owe it to ourselves to find out."

Fifteen

Livvy bit her lip as she watched Mason move toward her. When he stopped, the water only separated them by inches instead of feet. She should have known that coming here, and then sitting on the edge of the hot tub while Mason sat on the other side—bare torso, damp hair, wet skin—wouldn't help with her resolve to stay away from him. To stop thinking about kissing him. To forget how it felt to be in his arms.

He was gazing at her like a feline cat watching a shadow, waiting for the slightest movement in order to pounce. The desire in his eyes mirrored the desire that was already consuming her. Was Mason right? Did they owe it to themselves to find out how real this . . . distraction was? Was Felicity right? Should Livvy give Mason a chance, then deal with Slade later?

"I can't make any promises," she finally said. "And I don't want to mess up your writing plans."

"I can't make any promises either," Mason said, moving

another inch closer. "And I'll make my deadline even if I have to chain myself to a library table and feed myself through an IV."

Livvy smiled, and Mason smiled back.

And then he closed the distance. His warm, wet hands cradled her face. Her eyes slipped shut just as his mouth found hers. Their first kiss had been a frenzy of touching and tasting. This kiss was agonizingly slow. Mason explored her mouth as if he was memorizing her. She could feel the warm steam of the water radiating from his body. She clutched at his shoulders, knowing she was inches away from falling into the water, but not really caring.

She kissed him back, memorizing him as well while she melted into his warmth, which only made her crave him more. Slade had never kissed her like this, and she couldn't imagine he ever would. But all thoughts of Slade or comparisons to Mason fled as Mason's fingers skimmed her neck, then moved down her back.

"You're going to get me wet," she whispered against his mouth.

"Do you want me to stop?" he whispered back.

"No," she said, and she felt his smile all the way to her toes.

He kissed her again, giving in to her wish, and she moved her hands behind his heated neck, then through his damp hair. His hands skimmed along her sides and settled at her waist, where she could feel the imprint of his fingers through her clothing.

Then his kisses moved from her mouth to her jaw to her neck. "Did I tell you that you smell good?"

"I don't think so." Her words came out breathless.

"You smell good," he said. "And taste good."

She shivered at his words.

"Are you cold?" he asked, lifting his head.

She laughed. "Um, far from it. But I think we should slow this down . . ."

His smile was lazy. "Yeah, we should dry off and drink something really cold."

Livvy nodded and slowly, reluctantly let him go. She pulled her feet up and dried them with the towel, then she slipped her socks and shoes on. She stood and held open the towel. "Come on. You can give me a tour of your luxury cabin."

Mason climbed out of the hot tub and used the towel to rub his face and chest, then he wrapped it around his waist.

Livvy kept her hands to her side, trying not to stare at his lean, sculpted body.

Mason leaned toward her and brushed his lips against hers in a barely there kiss. "Thanks." He grasped her hand and linked their fingers together.

Then he picked up her coat, and she walked with him to the sliding glass doors of the cabin. Although heat still radiated from Mason's bare torso, he also had goose bumps from the cold temperature change, and she had to restrain herself from wrapping herself up in his arms to make the goose bumps go away.

Mason slid open the door, and she stepped through, her hand still in his. Mason entered after her and closed the door. The temperature inside the cabin was almost too warm compared to the cold from outside.

"The kitchen's through there," Mason said, pointing at the lit doorway on the other side of the great room. "You can put your shoes by one of the heater vents to get them dry. I'm going to get dressed, and then we can do the tour."

She nodded, and he released her hand.

Livvy stood still for a moment after he went up the stairs to whichever bedrooms were up there. It was a very good thing he was getting dressed, because Livvy was still craving his kisses. She'd kissed him more today than she'd kissed Slade in five months of dating. Was this an infatuation? Or was there more to whatever she was feeling toward Mason?

Her heart thundered as she thought about what it might be like to fall in love with Mason. To want him as her one and only. And then to lose him. Because he'd made it clear that he'd be returning to San Diego once his book was written. So where did that leave her?

Regretting that she hadn't held onto Slade? Or would she move on, completely Slade-free and Mason-free, and redefine all that she'd thought she wanted since she was a girl?

The sound of water rushing through pipes brought Livvy back into the here and now. Mason must be taking a shower, and Livvy refused to let her thoughts stray even further. She took off her damp shoes and set them by one of the heater vents, then she walked into the kitchen and found the cupboard with glasses. She filled it up with ice and water from the fridge. Mason was right. She needed something to cool her off and restore her senses.

Still, her skin thrummed with heat as she remembered Mason kissing her in the hot tub. She took her ice water into the great room and crossed to the gorgeous hearth. A flip of the switch made the gas fire come to life, and that's where Mason found her when he came back down the stairs.

"Are you warm yet?" he asked in that low voice of his.

She turned to see that he'd showered and dressed. He wore a light-gray T-shirt that looked as if it had been made to follow the line of his lean muscles in his arms and chest. His jeans were faded and sat low on his hips. *Oh boy.*

"I'm warm," she said.

Mason stepped to her, smiling as he scanned her face. She

hadn't even checked her makeup in the bathroom. Her mascara was probably smeared, and there were definitely no traces of lip gloss left. Mason took the ice water from her hands and took a long drink, then handed it back. "Want a refill?"

"I'm good."

He smelled like soap and musk, and his hair was still damp.

"So . . ." Livvy began. "Tour?"

"Yeah, that's right." Mason took her hand, and together they walked through the cabin. He flipped on lights as they went, and Livvy was both charmed at the beautiful workmanship and a bit envious. How would it be to have a *second* home like this?

They moved up the stairs, and Mason pointed out that the banister had to be custom carved. He seemed to notice details she didn't pick up.

"What's your house like in San Diego?" Livvy asked.

Mason paused at the top of the stairs. "It's an older home that I had remodeled the year I first hit the *New York Times* list."

"Is it in a neighborhood or by the ocean?"

Mason's mouth curved. "By the ocean. Premium property now that there's a lot of development going on. If I were to ever sell it, I'd definitely make a profit." He squeezed her hand.

Livvy's pulse skyrocketed. What did that hand squeeze mean? That he *would* consider selling his house to be close to her? She exhaled, telling herself not to jump to conclusions.

"My favorite part of this cabin is the fireplace in the master bedroom," he said. "Not that I've used it yet, but the ambiance is nice."

She walked with him through the three bedrooms, and

indeed, the fireplace in the master bedroom was a lovely addition.

As they headed back down the stairs, Mason said, "If you're not too tired, we could watch a movie or something."

Livvy should be tired. She guessed it was after 11:00 p.m., but she was wide awake. "I'm not too tired."

"Good," Mason said as they entered the great room. "There's no smart TV in the cabin, but there's a large selection of DVDs."

Livvy tugged his hand to stop him, then pulled him toward the couch. She sat down and he followed, his brows raised. "Or we could talk about your book," she said.

Mason's mouth quirked, then he leaned over and kissed her cheek. He didn't pull back, his breath warm on her face when he said, "I was hoping you had something else in mind."

She laughed. "Nope."

He kissed her on the mouth this time, one of his hands resting lightly on her neck as if he considered her a fragile thing. She indulged in the kiss for a few moments, then she drew away.

"Have you really never talked about your plot when you're writing?" she asked.

"Never." His blue gaze focused on her as he skimmed his thumb along her collarbone.

Ignoring her erratic pulse, she said, "What are you afraid of, Mason Rowe?"

"A lot of things," he said in a low voice. "Mostly I'm afraid of waking up one morning and realizing that I'm a horrible writer and all those nasty reviews are true and that I'll never finish another book again."

"Well, if that happens, you can sell your million-dollar home in San Diego, and move in with me," Livvy teased.

Mason winked. "I might do that anyway."

Okay then. Back on track . . . "It might help to talk about your story, you know. Not to get another person's ideas mixed in, but to sort it all out in your mind."

Mason stared at her for a moment with those gorgeous blue eyes of his, which were a darker color in the firelight. "Olivia Harmon, you are the most persistent woman I know. You might even outrank my agent."

Livvy laughed. "If that's a compliment, I'll take it."

"Given." He leaned in as if he was going to kiss her again, but she put her hand on his chest and felt the thump of his heart.

"Let me in, Mason. That's all I'm asking."

He trailed his fingers over her shoulder, then down her arm. "I'm trying to distract you, can't you see?"

"Believe me, you are distracting," Livvy said. "But like you said, I'm persistent."

Mason captured her hand and brought it to his lips. After pressing a kiss on her hand, he said, "I'll make you a deal. You tell me a deep, dark secret, and I'll tell you the name of my main character."

"That hardly seems like an equal trade," she said, although she was glad they were getting closer to a compromise.

"Take it or leave it." Mason turned her hand over and kissed her wrist.

She could let him kiss her all night or she could get to know this man better, so that she could decide if what was going on between them was real. And . . . if she told Mason her deepest secrets, then she'd know if he was a fight or flight person. "Okay. It's a deep, dark secret. And only Felicity knows. But I trust her enough to know she'd never betray me."

Mason's brows lifted. "Is it really a deep, dark secret if Felicity knows?"

"Take it or leave it."

"I'll take it," Mason said with a laugh.

"Okay, this is kind of hard to admit, so no laughing or teasing." Livvy pulled away from Mason so that she could look him in the eyes with a little distance from his tempting touch. "Ever since I was a little girl, my dream has been to marry a doctor."

Sixteen

$\mathcal{M}$ason wasn't sure he'd heard Livvy right. "You wanted to marry a doctor, no matter what?"

She bit her lip and looked away from him. "Yes."

Her voice was quiet, and at least she'd hesitated, but he'd heard her loud and clear. He was definitely not going to laugh at this. Was it still her dream? Her plan for her life? Not that he was about to propose to her, but . . .

Her gaze returned to his. "There was a family in my neighborhood where I grew up. The father was a doctor and the wife was beautiful. She ran all the charity events, she was the school PTA president, she wore gorgeous clothing. They had three boys, and those boys grew up to go to Ivy League colleges and, well, I wanted to be like the doctor's wife."

"And you carried that wish into adulthood?"

She nodded. "Thus the deep, dark secret."

Mason blinked. He wasn't sure how to read her. "Kids always have fantasies. What I want to know is if you are still living in that fantasy? Because I can guarantee you that Mr. and Mrs. Doctor didn't have the perfect life, no matter what it might look like from the outside."

"I know," Livvy whispered.

Mason tipped up her chin, and she met his gaze. What he saw in her eyes made his stomach sink. "Is that why you're dating Slade?"

She shrugged, and Mason dropped his hand.

"How many other doctors have you dated?" he asked.

She exhaled. "I dated two pre-med students in college. Slade is the first licensed doctor I've dated."

"And . . . you see him as the ticket to a perfect life?"

Livvy rubbed the back of her neck. "I know that no relationship is perfect. But I've held onto this fantasy, or dream, or goal, for most of my life." Her pleading gaze met his. "I told you my secret was dark."

"And twisted."

"Yes."

Mason looked toward the fireplace and the orange flames. "What does Felicity think?"

"She teases me about it mostly," Livvy said. "But when I told her what happened in the library between us . . ."

Mason snapped his gaze back to Livvy. This he hadn't expected.

"Felicity thinks I should . . . give *you* a chance."

He nodded. "So you came over tonight?"

"Not just because she suggested it, though," she said quickly. "I wanted to clear the air between us, and make sure you weren't mad or anything. But now I'm kind of sensing I've made you mad anyway."

"I don't think I'd call it mad," he said. "It's more surprised. You're a grown woman. You have a master's degree. You're an amazing person. Yet . . ."

"Yet . . . ?"

"I think that's for you to answer," Mason deadpanned. She tucked her feet under her. "Okay, the truth?"

At his nod, she continued. "I've wanted to marry a doctor my whole life," she said. "Even though I'd seen plenty of happy marriages out there, including my own parents, I wanted to be that woman in my neighborhood. Whenever a guy would ask me out, I'd ask him what he wanted to be after college. If he said anything other than a doctor, I wouldn't go out with him."

Mason wanted to laugh at the inanity of it all, but he'd promised not to. "So if Slade wasn't a doctor, you wouldn't be dating him?"

Livvy was quiet for a moment. "The old Livvy would have turned him down."

Finally they were getting somewhere. "There's a new Livvy now?"

Her gaze held his. "Until we kissed, I hadn't realized what I was missing."

Relief pulsed through Mason. "What have you been missing?" he asked in a low voice.

She touched his arm, then ran her hand up to his shoulder. Her warm fingers brushed against his neck, spreading tingles along his skin. "What it feels like to be desired by a man."

Mason stared into her brown eyes for a long moment. "Get used to it, Livvy Harmon."

She smiled right before he tugged her close and kissed her. Her arms went around his neck, and it was a heady feeling to have this woman fit so perfectly against him.

She broke off the kiss way too soon. "It's your turn," she whispered.

It took him a moment to come out of his haze to realize what she was saying. "Pilot," he said.

She pushed against his chest. "Pilot? That's his name, or he's a pilot?"

Mason didn't let her move another inch away. "That's his nickname, but I haven't decided what his real name is yet."

"Ah," she said. "And what sport does Pilot play?"

"Football." Mason groaned. "Uh, I didn't mean to say that. I promised to only tell you the character's name."

Livvy grinned. "Well, you still look like a bestselling thriller writer to me. I don't think anything has changed because you told me which sport Pilot plays."

He narrowed his eyes.

But she wasn't deterred. "Is he a quarterback? Receiver? Does he break his collarbone in a crazy tackle? Or maybe gets a concussion?"

Mason blew out a breath. "Are you trying to end my career?"

She leaned forward and gave him a soft kiss on his cheek. "No, I'm trying to get you to trust me, despite my dark secret of fantasizing about marrying a doctor." She ran a finger across his collarbone, then over his shoulder. "You know, we're kind of the same in that way. You have a strange fantasy that if you tell someone your plot, you're going to jinx your entire career."

Mason gazed at her for a long moment, debating. If he expected her to give up her fantasy, then maybe he should give up his superstition. "Pilot is the star quarterback for a college team. He breaks his hand, and he's supposed to sit out for five weeks. Which isn't a problem since it's the end of the season with only a bowl game to go. But when the second-string quarterback screws up in the fourth quarter, Pilot pops a couple extra pills and tells the coach to put him in. They win the game, but it's already too late for Pilot. He's addicted, and he can't let anyone find out." Mason stopped talking.

"Brilliant." Livvy grinned. "Thank you for telling me."

Mason felt numb. But maybe Livvy was right. The world hadn't stopped turning.

When she rose from the couch, he grabbed her hand to stop her. "Wait, where are you going?"

"I need to get some sleep, and so do you," she said. "Good night, Mason."

He scrambled to his feet, his heart in his throat. Why was he feeling at such a loss with her saying she had to leave? It was probably midnight, and it was the sensible thing for her to do.

She slipped on her shoes, then picked up her coat and fished out her car keys.

"Will the canyon road be okay?" he asked as he watched her getting ready to leave.

Livvy smiled. "The roads are plowed and sanded. Remember I drove here."

She walked to the front door, and Mason followed. He opened it for her and looked outside. It wasn't snowing.

"Let me know when you get home," he said.

She stepped up to him and tilted her head. "You're kind of a worrier."

"Get used to it." He snaked an arm around her and pulled her close, then lowered his head and kissed her. Her warmth and scent and softness were intoxicating. Livvy was right. She should really go home, because the longer she stayed, the more he didn't want to let her go.

He released her. "Good night."

After she left, he stood in the open doorway, watching the road long after her car disappeared into the night.

Eighteen minutes later, she called him. "I'm home."

"How were the roads?" he asked.

"Fine."

A heartbeat passed, and Mason thought of all the things he shouldn't be saying at this stage in their relationship. So he stayed quiet.

"I'll see you tomorrow?" she said.

"Of course."

She exhaled, and he imagined her smile. "Bring breakfast," she said.

"I was planning on it," he told her, smiling too.

When he hung up, he knew he wouldn't be sleeping for a while. So he grabbed his notebook and settled on the couch where he'd been sitting with Livvy and divulging his plot only moments earlier. In the orange glow of the fireplace, he began to write.

Hours later, he was awakened with a start. Thank goodness for the rumbling of the snowplow, or else Mason might have slept through the morning.

He sat up and rubbed the soreness in his neck. Apparently he'd written for hours, then fallen asleep on the couch. He glanced at the rough-hewn wood clock above the mantle, it was nearly 10:00 a.m. The library was open, and the muffins were probably gone from the Main Street Café.

Mason grabbed his cell phone. Nothing from Livvy. *Huh.* Hadn't she missed him?

He ignored the knot of worry that was beginning to form in his stomach. It was as Livvy had said; he was a worrier. He'd go get whatever was leftover at the café, then show up at the library and see her then. Mason didn't need to text or call her beforehand.

Forty minutes later, when he walked into the library and saw Livvy talking to another woman at the reference desk, he was relieved that she seemed to be okay. He browsed some of the nearby bookshelves while he waited for the other woman to leave.

He'd found an interesting book to flip through when Livvy suddenly appeared in the aisle.

"You're late," Livvy said, her brown eyes warm.

"I wrote most of the night, then slept in."

Livvy squealed and threw her arms about his neck. Mason almost lost his balance but thankfully didn't bump the bookshelf behind him. He chuckled and wrapped an arm about her waist, pulling her close.

"I told you that sharing your plot wouldn't ruin anything," she said.

Mason touched his forehead to hers. "And you were right."

She smiled and closed her eyes, so he kissed her.

It seemed they were kissing again in the library aisle.

She drew away much too soon. "There are a bunch of people here since it's not snowing."

Mason released her and stepped back. "Better hide this in your desk then." He held up the bakery sack.

"Thank you." She peeked in the sack. "Banana nut?"

"It was all they had left. Do you like that kind?"

"I like pretty much any type of food," Livvy said, then leaned into him, wrapping her arms about his waist.

He held her close and breathed her in.

They didn't say anything for a few moments, and Mason found that nothing needed to be said. Just holding her was enough for now.

When Livvy returned to the reference desk, Mason made his way to his usual table. Two teenagers occupied his spot. They must be homeschooled; otherwise he couldn't figure out why they were there this time in the morning.

He could do this though . . . write in a different spot . . .

Walking among the tables, desks, and shelves, he found a desk that faced a huge mural painting of a woman reading books to a circle of children sitting in the grass.

A memory flashed through his mind of his mom reading stories to him at night. He hadn't thought of that in a long time, and now it made him wonder if the early reading she did had somehow influenced his desire to write stories now.

He sat down and flipped through his notebook. His skin still buzzed from being with Livvy, and he decided it was time for Pilot to meet the woman who would be integral to his healing. A woman who would pick him up when he fell.

Seventeen

"I haven't told Mason about Thanksgiving with Slade's family," Livvy said into the phone.

Felicity sighed. "You might need a new strategy. I didn't think that things would be moving this fast with Mason."

"Me either." Livvy pulled the blanket on her bed over her. It was snowing outside again, and tomorrow was Thanksgiving. She and Mason had spent time together every night for the past week . . . and Livvy knew her heart was now involved.

She'd managed to put off seeing Slade, although she hadn't yet backed out on Thanksgiving with his family. Which she'd decided to do, but she still hadn't brought herself to cancel.

"I think you need to tell Slade before dinner with his family, because what if he does something like propose?" Felicity said.

Livvy scoffed. "He wouldn't do that . . . I mean, there's only been that one kiss." A kiss she could barely remember, since everything Mason had been consuming her thoughts. "I'll cancel on dinner, say I'm going to my family's after all. Then things can just sort of die between Slade and me."

Felicity's silence told Livvy that her friend didn't agree.

"That's not fair to Mason," Felicity said at last.

"I know." Livvy *did* know. And she wasn't trying to dangle both men . . . she was just dreading telling Slade that she'd been seeing Mason. Everything was great with Mason, except for the fact that he'd be returning to San Diego. Possibly before Christmas. Mason had written 200 pages of his book, and since his books were around 300 to 350 pages, it was like a giant ticking clock counting down.

"Tell Slade tonight," Felicity pressed.

Livvy moaned. "It would be so much easier to lie, but I owe him the truth. I don't want him hearing about Mason from someone else. We haven't been outed yet, but once I'm free of Slade, things with Mason could get more public."

"I could be your Cyrano de Bergerac," Felicity offered.

"That's why I love you, Felicity," Livvy said. "You're willing to dwell in the trenches with me." She glanced at the time on her phone. 7:00 p.m. Slade was on call tonight, but if he wasn't at the hospital, then he should be able to talk on the phone. *Or in person.* She sighed. "Okay, I'm leaving the house now and going over to Slade's place. Weirdly, Mason got invited to do something with Dawson Harris, and even more weirdly, Mason accepted. So . . . I can confess my horribleness to Slade, then wallow in guilt the rest of the night alone. Wish me luck."

Felicity gave a short laugh. "Good luck," she said with confidence that Livvy didn't feel. "And you can always come over to my place after for chocolate."

"Thanks," Livvy said, then hung up. She could do this . . . she *had* to do this. Mason was busy, and Slade was on call, probably sitting at his condo, waiting to be called into hero status again.

She left her bedroom and found her coat and boots. The snow was coming down pretty good now. Mallory had already left for the long weekend to be with her family, and Livvy would have Thanksgiving dinner with Felicity. Mason had insisted on sticking to his writing and frozen pizza. Maybe Livvy would surprise him with dessert.

She opened the garage and started up her car, then she drove slowly through the neighborhoods of Pine Valley. The snowplows weren't out yet since the snow was so new, and she guessed service would be slow anyway with the holiday.

Slade lived in a newer condominium community. He'd never talked about his plans to buy a house, but Livvy had never asked him either. She'd only been to his place once, and it was obvious the last thing on his mind was decorating. He had nice furniture, but nothing on the walls.

Livvy parked and climbed out of her car. The cars in the parking lot were already piled with a couple inches of freshly fallen snow. Livvy hoped this would be a quick exchange—or breakup—so she could make it back home before the town was buried.

When she reached Slade's door, she was surprised to see so many lights on. Voices were coming from the other side of the door—multiple voices—did he have people over? She couldn't appear on his doorstep when he had company and break up with him. Stepping away, she was about to turn and leave when the door opened.

Two men came out, laughing about something.

Livvy glanced back, then wished she hadn't. One of them was Slade.

Okay, so maybe his company was leaving and they could talk.

"Liv?" Slade said. "Hey, I didn't know you were coming over."

"Uh, yeah," Livvy said. "I thought I'd stop by since I was . . ." Her voice trailed off. "Is this your brother?"

Slade grinned. The man next to him looked a lot like Slade, but older, with a bit of a paunch belly and a much thinner hairline.

"Mike's in town for Thanksgiving and stopped over to watch the game, but his wife keeps texting him," Slade said.

Mike laughed. "You know wives." He elbowed his brother.

"Mike, this is Olivia Harmon," Slade continued. "Liv, this is Mike."

"Hi." Livvy felt like she had a rock in her throat, but she stepped forward and shook Mike's hand.

His hand was hot and clammy, and her hand was, well, cold.

"Great to meet you, Olivia," Mike said. His teeth were as white and straight as Slade's. "I've been wondering if my little brother was making up stories of his mystery girlfriend. Now I know you're real."

He and Slade laughed, and Livvy joined in, although her laugh burned her chest. How could she have thought showing up at Slade's unannounced would be a good idea?

"Well, see you tomorrow, Olivia," Mike continued. He leaned toward Slade and said in a stage whisper. "Mom's going to love her."

Slade actually blushed.

Livvy had never seem him blush or act self-conscious about anything. She'd also never seen him around his family. She wanted to run back to her car and drive home. Breaking up over texting was totally normal now, right?

"Hey, are you coming back in?" a woman said from the

doorway. "It's freezing out here." The tall, willowy woman had sleek brown hair that hung almost to her waist. Since she also looked quite a bit like Slade, she could only be his sister, Jessica. Her green eyes widened as her gaze met Livvy's.

"Oh, hi there." Her smile was wide and full of anticipation. "You're Liv?"

She nodded because her throat was suddenly dry.

"Yeah, we're coming in," Slade said. He placed a hand on her back, and she had no choice but to walk into his apartment.

"Nice to meet you at last. I'm Jessica," Jessica said. "We were all about to wring Slade's neck for not bringing you to our family dinners."

Livvy smiled despite the sick feeling growing in her stomach. Apparently everyone in Slade's family knew about her.

She moved past the entryway and into the living room where a football game was on, and the coffee table was littered with drinks and bowls of chips. Two other people were there, and Livvy recognized one of them.

"Hi, Sarah," Livvy said, and before she could ask what her connection was to Slade's family, Jessica answered her question.

"Oh, of course you know Sarah Lynne," Jessica said. "Sarah and I go *way* back. High school if you can believe it. Our boys are the same age, too."

Sarah smiled at Jessica. "And both boys are a load of trouble."

Jessica laughed. "True."

Livvy could definitely see the two women as friends. They had similar, graceful looks, and both had friendly personalities.

Slade draped an arm over her shoulder.

Livvy tried not to stiffen, but it was impossible to tamp down the embarrassed heat rising in her neck, because Sarah was looking directly at Livvy—with a knowing look in her eyes. Sarah had been a witness to Livvy and Mason's breakfasts at the café. Since that first breakfast Livvy had been to with Mason, they'd met there two other times. They'd never shown any affection in public, but Livvy knew that Sarah wasn't dense.

"Liv, I'd like you to meet Ben," Slade said, "who's married to my sister."

"Hi," Livvy said to the dark-haired man who had just risen from the couch. He stepped forward and shook her hand.

"Now it's a real party," Jessica said, all smiles. Another set of perfectly straight white teeth. "And Slade says more people are coming."

Livvy didn't know if she could handle any more people. Slade's family was plenty. *Please don't be his parents*, she silently begged. How would it be to meet his parents tonight, only to have Slade show up for Thanksgiving dinner tomorrow and announce their breakup? It was hard enough meeting his brother and sister.

Livvy wished that Sarah was a closer friend, then maybe she could pull Sarah aside and explain a couple of things. Instead she'd have to deal with knowing Sarah was probably judging her pretty harshly right now, and rightfully so.

"Are you hungry?" Slade asked. "We have pizza and salad in the kitchen."

"Not really—" Livvy started to say when Jessica clasped her arm.

"I'll show you," Jessica said. "Then we can have some girl time. I can't tell you how hard it is to get Slade to eat anything but rabbit food. He's such a health nut. But he says you like pizza."

Livvy breathed. "I do."

Jessica laughed. "What a relief. My brother's girlfriend is normal."

Livvy laughed too, but it was forced. Before she knew it, she was being tugged into the kitchen by Jessica.

Sarah joined them too. "Oh, good, a break from the men chest-pounding about their high school football days."

"Nothing is so important as high school football," Jessica said with a smirk.

Sarah laughed and shook her head. Livvy smiled, but it felt like she was moving mountains to do so. Normally the pizza would look delicious, but Livvy knew she couldn't eat a thing.

"So what kind of pizza do you want?" Jessica picked up a plate as if she was about to dish it up for Livvy. "Are you a pepperoni gal, or do you like the gourmet?"

"I'm not that hungry," Livvy said. "I'll just have a drink for now."

"All right," Jessica said, waving the plate. "If you're sure . . . ?"

Livvy nodded and poured a drink of soda and took a sip, as if to prove her point. "So where are you from?" she asked Jessica.

As Jessica talked, Livvy wondered how long she could make small talk before coming up with some excuse to leave. She could always use the weather, but everyone here probably had a car and would have to drive as well. And she didn't want to corner Slade into being gallant and saying he could take her home in his Land Rover later.

Livvy nodded at whatever Jessica was saying about her two kids. A daughter and a son.

"They've probably worn out Grandma and Grandpa by now," Jessica said. "I should text my mom."

Good. Livvy could use Jessica's momentum to leave to leave herself.

"Oh," Jessica said in the next moment. "They're watching *Moana* together. Adorable."

Sarah said something about how her son was obsessed with *Moana* too, when the doorbell rang. Livvy's stomach tightened as she heard new voices coming from the other room. Male voices.

And then everything around her stilled as she felt the blood drain from her face.

Mason was here. She also picked out Dawson's voice, which was loud and clear as he introduced Mason to Ben.

Slade said something, and everyone laughed.

Livvy looked toward the kitchen window. She could totally fit through it. Climb out and creep down the stairs. Jump in her car and leave.

"Well, sounds like Slade's lawyer friend is here, Sarah," Jessica said with a wink. "Is he as cute as you told me?"

Sarah flushed. "You can be the judge of that."

Jessica sighed a happy sigh. "Sometimes I miss the single days, but most of the time I don't."

Sarah laughed a bit nervously. "Dating with a kid is a whole other ball game."

Jessica nodded. "I'll bet." She looked at Livvy. "Well, let's go rejoin the men, shall we?"

What could she say? *I'll stay in here and eat.* Then make her window escape?

It seemed that Jessica was a very hands-on woman, and she linked arms with Livvy, steering her into the living room.

Slade sat perched on one of the arms of the couch. Ben sat on the other end of the couch. And Dawson and Mason were sitting in two chairs. Mason was leaning forward, his elbows resting on his knees, his eyes on the TV screen.

Livvy's heart went into overdrive as he looked up and their gazes met.

Eighteen

Mason hadn't wanted to come to Dr. Slade McKinney's place, but Dawson wouldn't take no for an answer. Which pretty much explained how Dawson had become the top lawyer in Pine Valley. He knew how to get his way.

"If Slade gets to know you, he'll drop his grudge," Dawson had said while Mason sat with him at the sports grill, eating barbeque sandwiches and watching the football game.

Mason hadn't answered.

"Slade will see you aren't out to steal his woman," Dawson persisted, "and you can bond over chips and pigskin."

Mason had wondered briefly what Dawson might say if Mason told him he'd already "stolen his woman."

But now, seeing Livvy walk into Slade's living room, Mason wondered if the joke was on him.

He couldn't help but stare. Mostly because it was so unexpected, and also because Livvy looked like she'd seen a ghost. Well, Mason felt the same way.

The brunette next to Livvy was a mirror image to Slade, and it wasn't a feat to discern that she was Slade's sister. She was also a chatterbox. She introduced herself as Jessica, first to Dawson, then she crossed to Mason and stuck out her hand. "I'm so excited to meet you," she gushed. "I'm not much of a reader, but I *so* respect your profession."

"I read," Ben said from the couch, lifting his hand and giving a little wave.

His wife smiled benignly at him. "I don't think *Sports Illustrated* counts, dear."

Ben chuckled.

Jessica once again cast her green-eyed gaze upon Mason. "So, have you met Sarah and Liv?"

Mason swallowed. He had yet to say one word.

"Of course he's met them," Slade said, having risen from his perch on the other end of the couch.

Mason watched as the doc moved to Livvy's side and slipped his arm about her waist. "Liv works at the library, and she's actually a big fan of thrillers, right, sweetheart?"

It was like a train wreck, and Mason couldn't look away as Slade leaned down and kissed Livvy's cheek. Her face stained red, and Mason didn't know if she was embarrassed about the public affection, or the fact that Mason was there to witness it.

On one hand, Mason was not naïve. He'd known almost from day one that Livvy had a boyfriend. And no matter what he might or might not have assumed, she'd never actually come out and said she'd broken up with Slade.

So. Mason slipped his phone from his pocket and sent a quick text to Jolene. *Call me ASAP.*

Jessica settled on the couch next to her husband, which put her in close proximity to Mason. "We hear that you're writing a book *right now*. What's it about?"

Mason's stomach flipped. "I, uh, don't really discuss works in progress. One of those weird writer quirks."

Jessica leaned closer and tapped a fake nail on his knee. "I won't say a thing. I mean, who would I tell anyway?"

Mason wondered if it would be rude to just walk out of the room. His phone rang, and he'd never heard a better sound in his life. He pulled it out of his pocket. "It's my agent. I'd better get this."

He rose to his feet, feeling Jessica's eyes on him. Livvy's eyes. Slade's. Dawson's.

"Hi, Jolene," he said into the phone as he strode toward the kitchen.

"Is everything okay?" Jolene said, worry in her voice.

"Yes, but I'll have to find a quieter place to talk. Hang on." He met Dawson's gaze. "Sorry, man. I've got to run." He looked to Slade, while at the same time he avoided meeting Livvy's eyes. "Thanks for the invite. Sorry I have to ditch."

He opened the door and walked out before the others could finish their goodbyes and good wishes. "Thank you," he said into the phone. "I think you saved my life."

"Mason, this isn't funny. What's going on?" Jolene did sound put out.

"Too complicated to explain," Mason said. "But happy Thanksgiving to you. I'll talk to you Friday, and I'll have a lot of writing news to report."

Jolene exhaled. "Fine. Happy Thanksgiving to you, too. Next time don't give me a heart attack."

Mason chuckled. "Deal." He hung up with Jolene and trudged through the snow to his Jeep. He was doubly glad he'd insisted on following Dawson's truck over to the condo complex. It sure made it convenient to escape.

The snow was coming down good, and Mason slowed his step as he passed by a red Honda. Livvy's. Most of it was covered by snow, and his first instinct was to tell her she shouldn't wait much longer to drive home. But he stifled that as soon as he thought it. Livvy wasn't his business anymore. He'd been a distraction, that was it.

Besides, by the looks of things, he wouldn't be surprised if Livvy spent the night at Slade's. She wouldn't have to drive at all. Surely the doctor had a fancy SUV of some sort.

Mason kicked at the pile of snow that had accumulated in front of his Jeep, then he set to swiping off the snow from the windows. The cold stung his hands, and he decided it felt good. He needed something to bite sense into him.

How had he let himself become so caught up in Livvy? How had he let his heart get away from him? Even now, he knew that if she came running out the door, he'd take her into his arms. He couldn't allow that. Words could deceive, but his very own eyes didn't lie.

Livvy might have been embarrassed that Mason had caught her with Slade. But Mason had seen enough in Slade's eyes to know that the doctor had intentions for Livvy. He wasn't going to let her get away. The stakes had been raised with Mason's arrival in Pine Valley. And Slade was up to the task.

Okay then. Mason yanked open the driver's door and hopped into his Jeep.

It was time to stop delaying on his book. Time to demand more from his muse and work her overtime. Time to ignore the cracking of his heart. Time to stop wallowing in the stress of the lawsuit. Mason had been found innocent, and Teddy guilty. Case closed.

Mason needed to close his heart and finish the damn book.

Once back at the cabin he decided the place was too quiet, and he flipped on lights, then synched his playlist to the

Bluetooth speaker. Music and lights would be a distraction. He silenced his phone and plugged it into a charger on the counter, face down so that if a certain person called or texted, he'd be oblivious. Next he grabbed his notebook, booted up his laptop at the kitchen island, and set to work.

Like he expected, the first paragraphs were painful, but then he got into a rhythm. He was typing too, not drafting by hand. Unlike in Mason's life, Pilot's girlfriend would stick around. She'd be the one to get him through the lowest of the lows. She'd see more in Pilot than he could see in himself. She'd stage an intervention, and she would be there every step of the way in his healing journey.

By the time Mason finished the intervention scene, his eyes were stinging with tears. He took a couple of deep breaths, saved the manuscript, then began the next scene, where the villain would begin his campaign to blackmail Pilot for everything he had. The words nearly typed themselves, and Mason had always found it ironic that when he wrote from the villain's point of view, the scenes unfolded like an intricate map.

It was the heroes who always pushed back. And the women. But women were always a different story.

Finally Mason knew he had to stop and take a break. Use the bathroom, get a drink, stretch his aching shoulders and neck. He downed a couple of ibuprofen before he checked his cell. The first thing he noticed was that it was 1:30 a.m. The second thing, Livvy had called three times.

No texts.

He stared at the Missed Calls icon listed by her name in his call log.

She hadn't left any messages. He hadn't even expected her to call. Maybe a text with an apology or *Can we talk?*

But when all was said and done, Livvy was a good person, a decent person. And an infuriating woman.

Mason slammed the phone on the counter, then immediately checked to make sure he hadn't cracked the screen. Apparently his cell phone was more resilient than his heart. He turned on the sound and decided if she called again, he'd answer. Might as well get the conversation over, and not that he felt like he owed her a conversation, but he knew on a psychological level closure was a good thing in the long run.

He walked to the couch in the great room, phone in hand, and sank onto the smooth leather. He let his head drop back against the cushion with a sigh. He'd known it was too good to be true, right from the beginning. Even when she'd kissed him in the library the first time, he hadn't let himself believe that there was a future for them. That he deserved more than he already had.

Sure, other people had relationships, and many of them the proverbial Happily Ever After. But that had never been his aim in life. Pilot would get his happy ending. And all of the heroes he had yet to write about would get theirs as well. That would be enough for Mason.

He picked up the phone. Livvy hadn't called back a fourth time. Even she had her limits, it seemed. Mason watched the time change on his phone.

1:42. 1:43.

He pressed Livvy's contact number. It rang once, then twice.

"Mason," she said into the phone. Her voice was thick with sleep, or had she been crying?

Mason's heart cracked a little more. "Hi."

"Thank you for calling me back," she said, her voice trembling.

Mason closed his eyes.

"Do you hate me?" she asked in a soft tone.

"I don't hate you," Mason said. And he realized he didn't. He couldn't.

"You probably won't believe me," she said, her hesitation evident, "and I don't deserve for you to believe me, but I went over to Slade's tonight to break up with him. Officially. I mean, I've been avoiding him since, well, since we've been together. Last week he invited me to Thanksgiving, and I accepted, thinking that maybe I'd know by then what was really going on with you and me. So I showed up there hoping he was home and not at the hospital . . ."

She continued to explain how the door had opened before she could make her escape and how she'd been drawn into the condo, then faced with meeting Slade's family for the first time. Mason could see it all playing out in his mind. Heck, he'd been there for some of it. And it was a pretty convincing story. True, sure. But that wasn't the point of what this conversation was going to be about.

"He cares about you, Livvy," Mason said in a tight tone when her words had run out. "I could see that tonight, and even though I still think he's an idiot, you two make a good pair."

"Is that what you really think, Mason?" The hurt was evident in her tone.

"I'm just calling it like I see it," he said. "Besides, he's a doctor. You know, your *fantasy.*" It was a low blow, and Mason regretted it the second he spoke.

"Screw you, Mason Rowe," she said in a fierce whisper.

Her anger was good, and he was happy she was angry, because he was angry too. And it would make all this easier. "I think it's better that we both admit this thing between us was a distraction, temporary . . . and agree to no hard feelings on either side."

Livvy didn't say anything.

"Go to Thanksgiving with his family," Mason said. "Figure out what *you* want."

"I hate this."

Mason couldn't agree more. "You're a smart woman, and I wish you all the best."

"Mason . . ."

He waited, but when she didn't say anything more, he said, "Goodbye, Livvy Harmon," then hung up.

It was over.

Nineteen

Livvy's eyes were swollen two times their normal size. She wasn't even sure she'd slept, even after she downed two Benadryl. Now she stared at her scary reflection beneath the buzzing florescent light in her bathroom. Seeing Mason's expression last night at Slade's would be something that would haunt her the rest of her life. If she'd felt guilty not telling Slade that she was seeing Mason, that was *nothing* compared to how she felt now.

She would have to tell Slade everything. If he forgave her, then some of the guilt might eventually go away. But Livvy didn't even want to see Slade today. She wanted to pound on Mason's door until he let her in and then beg for him to be the old Mason. Not the cold, distant Mason of last night.

She wanted to step into his welcoming arms. She wanted to feel his warm breath against her neck. She wanted him to kiss her. She wanted to feel his desire for her.

Livvy hated to think of how they'd be separated today.

Mason alone in that vast cabin. Livvy surrounded by Slade's entire family. She'd have to keep up her end of conversations, hold Slade's hand, smile at his parents, eat like she enjoyed the food . . .

Livvy decided she didn't like turkey either. She should have made the drive to her parents' home and avoided all of this. She grabbed a washcloth, soaked it with cold water, then pressed it against her eyes. Inhaling slowly, she decided she'd go to the dinner with Slade, and then tomorrow . . . she'd sleep all day. Mason was lost to her. And she didn't want Slade. Not anymore.

By the time Slade pulled up to her house, Livvy's puffy eyes were well concealed by an extra layer of makeup, and she'd decided she would enjoy Thanksgiving no matter what. She had plenty of things to be grateful for.

She wasn't even bothered that Slade was on the phone when she climbed into his Land Rover. He hadn't knocked on her door or opened the SUV door for her, but the call sounded important.

He seemed to be talking to a nurse by the medication orders he was giving. Five minutes into their drive, he hung up.

"Sorry about that, sweetheart."

Sweetheart. He'd called her that in front of Mason. "What's going on?" she asked, hoping her voice didn't sound annoyed.

"Oh, Mr. Palmer is in more pain than usual today," Slade said smoothly. "I told him day three after surgery would be the worst, but the nurse said he's really suffering. So I'm increasing the next dose."

"Poor man," Livvy said. "How old is he?"

"Seventy-two," Slade said. "Young enough to still get a lot of use out of his new back." He continued to talk about the surgery and aftercare, and normally Livvy would stay engaged, but she found her mind was wandering.

Was Mason heating up a frozen pizza? Had he gotten any writing done today? Would he tell his agent about their breakup? Had it *been* a breakup? It had felt like one, and here Livvy was with Slade again.

His phone rang, and he answered.

Livvy fisted her hands and stared out the window, watching the snowy landscape speed by. Slade had told her his parents lived on a ranch just outside the city proper, but Livvy hadn't ever been there.

"Put on Mr. Palmer," Slade said. "Maybe if I talk to him, and explain what's going on, it will ease his anxiety level."

Maybe Livvy should be driving.

Ten minutes later, Slade got off the phone just as they reached a turnoff that led to a ranch-style house on a large piece of property. The house and red barn, surrounded by horse property, looked like a scene on a winter postcard. Wow. When Slade had complained about living on pennies during medical school, she'd thought of his parents living in a much more modest home than what spread out before her.

"Here we are," Slade said in a bright voice as he parked the Land Rover next to someone's truck. He turned off the engine and opened his door.

Livvy didn't wait for him to come around, so she was already standing on the circular driveway when Slade reached her.

He smiled that perfect smile. "Ready?"

"Yep," Livvy said simply. For better or for worse.

Slade grasped her hand. His hand was smaller and smoother than Mason's, and Livvy didn't feel the same fluttering that she did when Mason took her hand. Of course when Mason did that, he usually kissed her too.

Livvy's stomach knotted at the thought of Slade kissing her again. There was a time a few weeks ago when she was looking forward to it, but now . . . She'd rather be having a quiet dinner with Felicity than with Slade's family.

The ranch house was beautiful, Livvy had to admit. And from the moment they stepped into the warm, glowing interior, Livvy was swept into one hug after another. She'd had no idea that Slade's family would be so welcoming and affectionate. Jessica hugged her like they'd been best friends for years, and Slade's mom, an older copy of Jessica, hugged Livvy as well without any reservation.

By the time everyone gathered in the large dining room, Livvy's mind was spinning. Slade's father said grace over the food, then excused all the grandkids to sit at a special table decorated just for them. Livvy sat between Slade and Jessica. During the meal, Slade's married siblings teased him about waiting so long to bring Livvy around.

And Slade's parents kept smiling at her.

More than once, Livvy's heart skipped a beat when she remembered how Felicity had teased her about getting proposed to by Slade at his family dinner.

She took small peeks at him and decided that not even Slade would be so brash.

"So tell me more about the thriller writer who's working on his book at your library," Jessica said, her voice a low purr. "He seems like a brooder. Kind of a loner, if you ask me. Can he carry a normal conversation, or does he live inside his head most of the time?"

Livvy had to choose her words carefully. First, because it was Slade's sister asking her, and second, Slade could hear every word she said.

"There's not a lot of conversation at the library," Livvy said.

"Oh, right," Jessica said with a laugh. "Those *Keep Quiet* signs and all."

"This food is so amazing," Livvy said, trying to steer the topic away from Mason. "If my mom was here, she'd be asking for recipes."

"What's your mom like?" Jessica asked.

Livvy decided that her mom might not have been the best detour, because everyone at the table fell silent as she gave a brief sketch of her parents and her younger brother.

Slade's phone rang while she was talking, and he excused himself.

"The doctor's always in demand," Slade's mother said, affection in her tone, and everyone around the table laughed.

Thankfully the conversation turned to the grandkids and their antics. Livvy hadn't eaten much, but she felt more than full. She sipped at her water while she wondered how long Slade was going to be.

"You'll have to see the photo albums of Slade when he was in high school," his mother crooned. "Always a straight-A student. Now Jessica, on the other hand—she made sure she enjoyed every moment."

Everyone laughed while Jessica pretended to glower. Livvy smiled politely. Slade's family was great, but the sick feeling in her stomach wouldn't subside. Her guilt was eating her from the inside out. And even when she did confess to Slade, she knew it wouldn't be to get him to forgive her and stay together. And it wouldn't be because she thought Mason would take her back.

She knew she'd be making a clean break. From both men.

"Hey, sweetheart," Slade said close to her ear.

Livvy turned to look up at him.

He had that puppy-dog look in his eyes. "I really hate to say this, but I've got to get to the hospital. I think I can be out of there in about an hour, then I'll come back here just in time for pie."

Heat shot through Livvy.

"If you have to stay longer," Jessica piped up, "Ben and I can take her home."

"Okay, I have no problem with that," Slade said, squeezing Livvy's shoulder. "What do you think, Liv?"

Livvy's hands started shaking. "Um, we'll see," she said in a too-bright voice. "I'll walk you to your car, and we can talk about it."

Slade frowned. "I've got to leave now though."

Livvy scooted her chair back. She didn't want to tell Slade that she wasn't going to be left behind with his entire family listening in.

Slade was still frowning. "Everything okay?" he asked in that concerned-doctor voice of his.

"Great," Livvy said, forcing a smile. "We can talk outside."

His brows lifted, and everyone at the table had fallen silent.

So awkward.

Livvy had no idea where her coat had ended up, and she didn't want to ask for it because then she'd have to announce that she was leaving with Slade. All she wanted to do was disappear.

She'd come to this dinner thinking . . . Well, she didn't know what she'd been thinking. But it wasn't to be left at the mercy of his family, as if she needed to be entertained, while Slade ran off to play doctor.

Slade's coat was hanging on a rack by the door, and when he picked it up, thankfully, there was her coat too. She grabbed it.

Slade said nothing, but opened the front door.

"What's this all about, Liv?" he said as they walked to the Land Rover.

"I want you to take me home, Slade."

He stopped and turned to face her. "Hey, I won't be gone that long. I promise. My family is so excited that you're here."

"It's not how long you'll be gone," Livvy said, folding her arms. "And you have a great family, but I'm finished with being the last person on your list."

Slade stepped back as if she'd physically pushed him. "What are you talking about?" His phone rang, and he had the audacity to fish it out of his back pocket and look at the screen. "Hey, can we talk about this later tonight? I've really got to get to the hospital."

"We can talk on the way to my house," Livvy said, moving toward the Land Rover and opening the passenger-side door. "You won't lose more than a few minutes by dropping me off. Either that or I'm calling a taxi."

Slade blinked. "Jessica said—"

Livvy had already climbed in and shut the door, cutting off his words.

Slade didn't move for a moment, then he hurried to the driver's side. He said nothing as he started the engine and pulled around the circular driveway. When he turned onto the road, he fiddled with the heater controls, then sped up as they reached the main road.

Livvy couldn't ever remember seeing Slade mad. In fact his mild manner with everything was annoying, when she thought about it. It was like he was always on the same emotional wavelength. No ups or downs. Always apologizing. She was so tired of hearing him tell her he was sorry.

Ironic, since she should be the one telling him.

But she wasn't sorry. Not anymore.

They were about ten minutes into their drive when Livvy said, "What do you like about me, Slade?"

"What?" The word was clipped.

"Just tell me one thing you like about me."

She felt Slade's incredulous gaze on her, but was the question really too hard to answer? She tried to think of any compliments that Slade might have given her over the past five months, and she came up empty.

He slowed at a stoplight. No one was at the intersection, and soon the light turned green. Slade accelerated. "Your eyes are pretty."

Livvy stared straight ahead. *Okay . . .* The seconds ticked by. "Is that all? You like my eyes?"

Slade exhaled. "You kind of sprung this on me. And you said *one* thing. Do you want a list or something?"

"No," Livvy said in a faint voice. Her eyes burned, and her throat ached. Only a few more streets to go. If the temperature were any warmer, she'd tell him to drop her off at one of the corners so she could walk.

He didn't even pull into her driveway but stopped at the curb.

"You know my mom's going to be upset," Slade said. "Pies are her specialty."

Livvy put her hand on the door handle, then looked over at him. "Then go back there, Slade. If you aren't going to put *me* first, at least put your family first. They love you, and they're proud of you."

Slade stared at her.

"Don't worry about walking me to the doorstep," Livvy continued. "I've got it. Just do me one favor. Don't call me again." She popped open the door and stepped down from the Land Rover.

"Liv . . ." Slade said. His tone wasn't quite pleading . . . more incredulous. Disbelieving.

She shut the door and walked to her doorstep. Before she could even unlock it, Slade peeled out from the curb. That's when her tears finally fell.

Twenty

The football game had been on for two hours, but Mason remembered none of it. He'd eaten half of a frozen pizza, then tossed the rest. He finally settled for snacking on a bowl of pistachio nuts. It wasn't the best Thanksgiving he'd had, but it also wasn't the worst.

His mother had been in the hospital the final Thanksgiving of her life. He and his dad had gone to visit her. Mason still remembered sitting on a hard chair in the corner of the tiny hospital room while his mother picked at some limp turkey on her food tray.

"Do you want this, Mason?" she'd asked.

"I'm not hungry," he'd said. "You can have it."

"Eat the turkey, son," his father had said. "Your mother wants you to have it."

Mason hated it when his dad called him *son*. It wasn't an endearment, but more of a power play on words. So Mason took the tray, and with both of his parents watching, he ate the turkey.

Now he couldn't think of turkey without thinking of his mom's thin and frail body in that hospital bed. Her blue eyes rimmed in red as she watched him eat. It was as if she knew . . . knew that she'd leave this life in only a few days' time.

Mason muted the football game and closed his eyes. This Thanksgiving might have been different if things had worked out with Livvy. He shook his head at the irony. She'd originally invited him to Thanksgiving with her and Felicity, but he'd turned her down. And now here he was . . . still alone.

Mason was half-asleep when someone knocked on his door. At first he thought he'd dreamed it, but then the knock sounded again. He looked at the rustic wood clock. It was about 8:00 p.m., so not all that late. But still . . .

He rose, and despite his reluctance to hope, he wondered if it was Livvy. Maybe the dinner with Slade's family had been a disaster, and she'd come to beg him for another chance. But even as he imagined it, he knew it wouldn't happen. With or without Slade between the two of them, Mason would be leaving Pine Valley soon.

He opened the door and blinked. "Dawson?"

"Hey, man," Dawson said, holding up a white bakery box. "Thought I'd come to make some peace. Apologize, you know, food-style."

Mason didn't move for a moment. "What are you doing here?"

Dawson moved past him anyway, walking into the cabin uninvited. "Nice place." He continued to the kitchen.

Mason stared after him.

"Hope you like banana cream pie," Dawson said. "They were all out of the traditional pumpkin."

Mason shut the front door, then joined Dawson in the kitchen as he lifted the lid of the box.

166

Mason recognized the Main Street Café logo. "The café was open tonight?"

"Uh, no," Dawson said. "Sarah Lynne let me in."

The twinkle in Dawson's eyes told Mason that it must have been a personal favor. He moved to the utensil drawer and pulled out a couple of forks. Then he found two plates and set them on the counter.

Dawson shed his long trench coat and settled onto a barstool as if he owned the place.

Mason joined him and dug into the pie. He might hate turkey, but he'd never turn down an offer of pie.

"So . . ." Dawson started. "Sorry about the other night. I mean, I didn't know that you and Livvy were, uh, together."

"We're not together," Mason said, then took another bite of the pie. The smooth and sweet creaminess was delicious.

Dawson scoffed. "The tension between the two of you in Slade's condo could have been cut with a dull plastic knife."

"Livvy's a great person, but she's with Slade, and well, I'm not planning on becoming a Pine Valley resident." Mason took another bite. "Although if they had a bakery like the Main Street Café in San Diego, I'd be in heaven."

Dawson laughed. "I'm glad you like the pie, but I think you're selling Pine Valley short."

Mason met Dawson's gaze. "Why's that?"

The man had a sly look on his face, which was dangerous considering he was a lawyer by occupation. "I just think you shouldn't discredit us quite so fast."

Mason scooped another forkful of pie but didn't eat it. "I'm listening."

"There's the Christmas Caroling night the week before Christmas," Dawson said.

Mason raised his brows. "Sounds cold."

"We wear coats and gloves and hats," Dawson said. "The

Main Street Café serves hot chocolate, and we gather around portable fire pits and sing Christmas songs. Then Santa visits the library and reads *The Night Before Christmas* to the kids. The librarians hand out candy canes and bookmarks."

Mason ate more pie.

"The library runs a charity drive in January," Dawson continued. "To raise money for the women's shelter and to pay for the book mobile runs to the assisted living center."

"I'm sensing a theme here; what happens in February in Pine Valley?" Mason said in a dry tone.

"Ah, that's the best month of all," Dawson said. "It's Valentine's, you know, and the bookshop runs a two-for-one sale. Store patrons are also given the chance to donate their purchases to the library. Cool, huh?"

Mason tried not to smile.

"And if you're around in March, the snow starts to melt, and the mountain slope behind this cabin will be covered in wildflowers. Makes for some great writing inspiration in your backyard, you know, if you like to soak in the beauty of nature while you follow your muse."

Mason smirked and rubbed his jaw. "April?"

"April is like the holy grail of the year. It only rains a handful of days, and the library hosts various authors to do a weekend-long literacy event."

"I'm sure it does, but I think I'll have met my writing deadline way before then," Mason said.

"For your current book," Dawson said with a nod. "But don't you have to write a book every year?"

Mason rose from the barstool and opened the fridge. He pulled out a half gallon of milk, then he poured two glasses and slid one over to Dawson. "Despite all these distracting events in Pine Valley, there are too many busybodies here who like to get into other people's business."

Dawson laughed. "Sometimes that can be an advantage."

Mason took a drink of his milk. "How so?"

"Let's just say that when Sarah Lynne was so kindly ringing up this pie for me when the café was closed, she happened to mention she'd been at the hospital visiting her neighbor Mr. Palmer."

Mason had no idea who Mr. Palmer was or what it had to do with him. "And?"

"She paused outside Mr. Palmer's door when she heard our Dr. Slade talking to him," Dawson said. "She didn't want to interrupt, so she waited. Mr. Palmer asked the good doctor how his Thanksgiving had been."

Mason wished he hadn't eaten all that pie. He wasn't feeling so well.

But Dawson didn't seem to notice. "Slade said Thanksgiving was perfect, up until his girlfriend dumped him."

Mason set his milk on the counter, carefully, since he didn't trust his grip. "You're kidding."

Dawson grinned. "Thought that might interest you." He pushed away from the counter and reached for his coat. "I should run. You can keep the rest of the pie."

Mason felt like he was in a haze as he watched Dawson shrug into his coat, then stride to the front door.

"See you around, Mason." Dawson opened the door and disappeared into the night.

Mason stared at the closed front door, realizing he hadn't even told the guy thanks. For the pie or for the information about Slade getting dumped. Mason didn't move from his place leaning against the counter for several moments. Then he began to clean up the dishes. He washed the glasses, plates, and forks, then dried them with a dishcloth.

So Livvy had dumped Slade.

It wouldn't change anything for Mason though. He'd still

be finished with his book in a few weeks, and he'd still be returning to San Diego. Livvy would probably start dating another doctor . . . Or maybe her fantasy had been blown wide enough apart that she'd date someone like Dawson.

Mason dried his hands and put the half-eaten pie into the fridge. What Livvy did or didn't do was no longer his business. He flipped off the kitchen lights and went back into the great room. Picking up his phone from the coffee table, he checked for any missed calls or texts. Nothing.

He turned on the fireplace, then booted up his laptop. He scrolled back through the last pages he'd typed up. He was glad he'd moved past the handwriting stage. Too slow. The sooner he was done with the book, the better.

The words came slowly, but they were coming, and Mason was startled out of a half-conscious existence when his phone rang. "Hi, Jolene," he said into the phone.

"Happy Thanksgiving," she said. "How is everything going?"

"Fine. Ate some pie. Now I'm writing."

"Really?" The relief in her voice was palpable. "That's great, Mason. Anything I can help you with?"

"No, I'm good." Mason paused. "How was your Thanksgiving?"

"Chaotic," Jolene said with a laugh. "Uncle Bill nearly choked on his food. My aunt dropped the turkey when she was carrying it to the table. Two of my cousins got into a fight about which season of *Supernatural* is the best. Usual stuff."

Mason smiled. "Sounds like a fun night."

"Definitely memorable," Jolene mused. "Hey, I got an email today from the owner of the cabin. He's wondering if you'll still be leaving before Christmas or if you need to extend. He has another person interested in renting during the Christmas season."

"You can tell him I'll be out before Christmas," Mason said.

After hanging up with Jolene, Mason returned to his story. The words came faster now, but his mind was only half in it. Mason wasn't complaining about his Thanksgiving, and Jolene's sounded like it was something he could have passed on. But he was sure Livvy considered hers a bust. She hadn't gone home to her family. As far as he knew, she'd gone with Slade, but then what had happened to make her dump him?

Had she dumped Slade *before* the dinner? *At* the dinner? After? The fact that Slade had been at the hospital in the first place might be another clue.

Mason closed his eyes as he wondered what Livvy might be going through right now. Her roommate was out of town. Maybe she was hanging out with her friend Felicity. Or maybe she was alone at home. Mason exhaled. Whatever Livvy was doing, it wasn't his business. He refocused on the laptop screen.

By 10:00 p.m., he'd written eight more pages, but he was losing his concentration. Sure, he was tired, but he'd pushed through exhaustion plenty of times.

He wondered what Livvy might say if he called her. Just to check up on her. Would she tell him about the breakup? Would she even answer her phone?

There was only one way to find out.

Twenty-one

*L*ivvy had been watching Netflix for about three hours straight, and she couldn't have told anyone what she'd heard or seen if offered a million dollars. She'd fielded calls from her mom wishing her a happy Thanksgiving, another from Felicity, who got to hear the whole sob story, then a third call from Slade. That one she let go to voicemail.

Slade's voice had sounded exasperated in his message: "Hey, I'm leaving the hospital and wanted to see if you can talk through some things. I don't know exactly what happened on the drive back from my parents, but I can assure you that you're *not* at the bottom of my list. Oh, hang on. I'll call you right ba—"

His message had cut off, and Livvy had laughed, then she'd cried. Then she'd texted Slade: *What part of Do Not Call Me do you not understand? We're done talking. I wish you all the best in your future. If I ever get admitted to the hospital, I'll say hi.*

So maybe that last sentence had been unnecessary. But it had felt good. She'd turned down Felicity's offer of hanging out. Livvy needed to wallow by herself. Besides, Felicity had to get up early for Black Friday sales at the bookshop. And Livvy was planning on watching Netflix until she dropped off to sleep on the couch.

She was in a half-stupor, binge-watching numbness when Mason's name lit up the screen of her phone. Livvy shot to her feet and stared down at her phone. Surprise, curiosity, hope, and nerves all collided inside her heart. Why was he calling her? Maybe he was leaving Pine Valley and was giving her the courtesy of saying goodbye? Or . . .

She picked up the phone. "Hello?" Her voice sounded too high, too breathless.

"You answered," Mason said.

Livvy brought a hand to her heart and closed her eyes. Just hearing his voice made her hurt all over again. "Did you want to leave a message? I can hang up and—"

"No." Mason's voice was low. "I was worried about you."

She puffed out a breath and sank onto the couch. "What are you worrying about?"

"I can't exactly pinpoint it," he said. "It's just a feeling."

Livvy blinked against the burning in her eyes. "You should be focusing on your book and everything you have going on. You don't have to worry about me."

"Yeah, that's what I keep telling myself," Mason said. "But then somehow I ended up calling you."

She smiled although she felt more like crying. "How was your pizza?"

"About as good as frozen pizza can get, although I wasn't all that hungry."

"I wasn't hungry for dinner either." Livvy pulled her feet up on the couch and tucked them under a crocheted throw that Mallory had made. "It's kind of hard to enjoy a meal when everyone is watching you, assessing you, even judging you."

"I'm sure Slade's sister was friendly," Mason deadpanned.

A laugh burst out of Livvy, and she kept laughing until she was practically crying.

Mason laughed with her.

When Livvy could finally breathe normally, she said, "I dodged a bullet there."

"You mean you aren't besties planning on going Black Friday shopping tomorrow?" Mason asked, his voice teasing, but Livvy sensed the question there.

"That will never happen," she said, her tone sober. "I broke up with Slade."

Mason didn't say anything for a minute. When he spoke, his words made her smile. "Do you need some words of consolation?"

"Not unless you want to give them," she said.

"I think my words of consolation would be more along the lines of 'I'm sorry it took you so long to dump the bas—'"

"Okay, okay, I get it," Livvy said with a laugh. "You've definitely never held back your opinion of him."

She could imagine Mason smirking.

"Are you all right, Livvy?" he asked.

Goose bumps broke out on Livvy's skin at the concern and gentleness in his tone. "Your phone call is helping."

"I can bring you some pie," Mason said. "I've heard that eating rich desserts can ease the pangs of the heart."

"Oh really?" she teased. "You don't like turkey, but you like pie?"

"I'd be an idiot not to like pie." He paused. "I can drop it off on your porch if you don't want to see me."

Livvy's pulse hummed. "Answer me this one question,

Mason . . . even if you sort of hate me right now, what did you like about me when, you know, we were hanging out?"

There was no hesitation when he spoke. "I don't think I could ever hate you, Livvy Harmon. And I like a million things about you. Like how you are nosy and how you ask prying questions and how you won't take no for an answer."

She smiled.

"I like the way your hair curls and how you always smell like cinnamon," he said. "I like how you've read all of my books and force me to talk about my current manuscript. I like how you've seemed to cure my writer's block."

Livvy's skin heated. "You can't give me credit for that."

"I'm not finished," Mason said, a smile in his tone. "I like watching you run the library, being equally bossy and helpful at the same time. And I like that you still seem to have no idea how to dress properly for winter weather."

She laughed. "I just avoid being outside."

"But mostly I like the way you kiss me."

Livvy's heart skipped a beat. "That's a lot of likes," she said in a soft voice. "Maybe you should bring that pie over."

"See you soon." Mason hung up.

Livvy stared at the phone a few seconds, her mind reeling. When she'd asked Slade what he liked about her, he had told her one thing—*her eyes.* But when she'd asked Mason . . . She jumped up from the couch. He was coming over. *Now.*

She straightened up the room, folded the crocheted blanket, fixed the throw pillows, then took her tea mug to the kitchen. She did the few dishes there and wiped down the counters. Then she hurried to the bathroom and brushed her teeth. She checked the time. It had been eight minutes, and her face was a blotchy mess.

She scrubbed her face, then reapplied some mascara and

added lip gloss. Next she went into her bedroom and changed out of her yoga pants into jeans and a V-neck sweater. She didn't want to be too dressed up, but she didn't want to look like she'd been bingeing on Netflix for three hours. She was still in the bedroom when a knock sounded at the front door.

Her heart nearly leapt out of her chest.

Mason was here. And she hoped this meant things between them could be . . . good again? Friendly? He'd still be leaving Pine Valley, and she'd have to deal with that at some point. But at least she didn't have two men hating her tonight. Slade she could deal with, but she didn't want Mason hurt.

Livvy smoothed back her hair. It was too late to do anything with it. She walked to the front door, glancing at the living room. She grabbed the remote and clicked off the TV. Then she reached for the doorknob.

Sure enough, Mason Rowe was on her doorstep, a white box in his hands.

"You really do have pie," Livvy said.

"You thought it was a ruse?" His gaze moved from her face to her sweater, then lower.

Livvy was glad she'd improved her appearance.

Mason wore a dark shirt layered with another thick flannel shirt. His jeans were the ripped ones she'd first seen him wearing at the library. He hadn't shaved for a couple of days, and Livvy decided that she liked all versions of Mason.

"I believed you." She pulled the door open wider. "You can come in, unless you'd rather leave the pie on the porch."

Mason chuckled and walked into her house. His sleeve brushed against her arm, and she ignored the warm shiver that trailed up her skin. She shut the door, and before she could tell Mason where to take the pie, he'd walked into her kitchen.

"You must like yellow?" he observed.

Seeing Mason standing in her rather small, brightly

painted kitchen was sort of amusing. He took up most of the space, and the dark colors of his clothing made the yellow walls and painted white daisies look like a baby nursery.

"I do like yellow, if you must know."

Mason's blue eyes met hers; his were amused.

She took the pie box from his hands and set it on the kitchen table, then grabbed two forks. She handed him one.

He waved it off. "I've had enough pie."

"So you're just going to watch me eat?"

He nodded.

She opened the lid and found a half-eaten banana cream pie. She perched on the edge of the table and scooped out a forkful, then ate it. "Mmm. You got this from the café?"

"Dawson brought it over." Mason leaned against the edge of the table so that they were only a few inches apart.

She turned, brushing against him to get another forkful. He was kind of in the way, but she wasn't going to complain. "That was nice of Dawson," she said, and ate another bite.

"I suppose it was, but Dawson also had an agenda."

Livvy didn't know if she liked the sound of that. Dawson had been the one to warn Mason away from her. Dawson and Slade went way back.

"He told me that you dumped Slade," Mason said.

Livvy froze. "He did? How did he know?"

She listened as Mason told her everything Dawson had shared. At the end of it all, she said, "So . . . that's why you called me?"

"Sort of."

Livvy's heart sank. Mason hadn't called her because he couldn't stand being apart from her. He'd called because he'd already known she'd broken up with Slade. Mason was only being a friend. She straightened from the table. It didn't matter. Mason had been . . . a distraction. She had known that going in.

"That's why I *dared* to call you," Mason said, grasping her wrist and taking the fork out of her hand.

She met his blue gaze, but then she had to look away.

"I would have eventually called you, though," he said in a quiet voice.

Her throat was so tight it hurt. "To say goodbye."

Mason exhaled. He still hadn't released her wrist, and now, with his other hand, he touched her chin and lifted it.

She blinked against the burning in her eyes and met his gaze.

"I would have eventually called you because as you know, I'm a worrier," he said. "And apparently it's too hard for me to stay away from you."

Livvy didn't know whether to kiss him or to cry. She released a trembling breath. "So now what?"

"You tell me," Mason whispered, leaning down, his mouth inches from hers.

"I hope it takes you twenty years to finish your book," she said.

Mason's mouth curved, then he brushed his lips against hers.

The touch of his warm mouth sent darts of heat through her, and every part of her body ached to be near him. She gripped his shoulders and kissed him back. At last his arms were around her again, and she was right where she wanted to be.

Twenty-two

Mason had become accustomed to every sound in the library. The slow hiss as the heater kicked on. The faint squeak of the front doors when they opened. The quiet rasp of the books as Livvy or Mallory replaced or organized the books on the shelves. The tapping of the keyboards at the reference computers. The rise and fall of the library patrons' whispers.

So when he heard the soft tread of tennis shoes coming up behind him, he had no doubt that Livvy was trying to surprise him. That, and he could smell roast beef. She must have brought him lunch.

Before she could touch him or say a word, he reached his arm back and grabbed a leg.

Livvy yelped, and he laughed, then tugged her onto his lap.

Her smiling face came into view, and her arms slipped around his neck.

"How did you know it was me?" she whispered.

"I have very keen senses," he said, taking the sack from her hand and setting it on the table behind her.

She gazed at him with those beautiful brown eyes of hers. Mason wanted to take twenty years to finish writing his book too, but in truth he was only a couple of chapters away from the final climax. Then it would be smooth sailing from there.

"Come here," he whispered.

"We're in the library."

"That hasn't stopped you before," he said.

Livvy's cheeks flushed pink, and she bent a little closer.

Mason tugged her the rest of the way and kissed those berry lips of hers. Her fingers moved into his hair, then he ran his hands down her back.

The front door to the library squeaked open, and Mason drew back. It would only be seconds before whoever had entered would be able to see the librarian sitting on his lap, kissing him.

Livvy seemed to realize this in the next moment and leapt from his lap.

Mason chuckled softly as she set the sack of food under the table, then brought her finger to her lips. "You can eat in the back room if you'd like," she said, then moved away to see if whoever had entered the building needed any help.

Mason waited a few minutes, then he picked up the sack of food and carried it to the back room that doubled as a storage room and sort of office. A small fridge sat in the corner where Livvy kept drinks, so he grabbed a water bottle. He'd donate to the library fund later, or just bring in another case of water bottles. There was much to be desired in the cramped space, but Mason wasn't all that picky. He'd rather write in this library, close to Livvy, than stay in the million-dollar rented cabin.

His thoughts turned to the cabin. It was now mid-December, which meant he had less than two weeks. He and Livvy hadn't technically discussed his leaving date, and he knew they were both putting off that conversation. They should probably get it over with.

Would they try the long-distance thing for a while? Then let it fade?

"Hey you," Livvy said, coming into the back room.

"This is great, thanks," he said. "I saved some for you."

She waved him off. "I ate my turkey sandwich."

Mason grimaced.

"Are you ever going to tell me why you hate turkey?" she asked, walking toward him, then slipping her arms about his waist.

He looked into those warm brown eyes of hers. Eyes he trusted. Eyes he cared about. "It's one of those long, sad stories."

Her smile was soft. "I still want to hear it."

"Okay," he said. "Maybe tonight when you come over to my cabin and we're in the hot tub together."

Livvy laughed. "Sounds like a bribe."

Mason winked. "As always, swimsuits are optional."

He loved it when she blushed.

Mason leaned down and kissed her forehead. "As much as I love being distracted by you, I've got to get my pages in. You can eat the rest of that sandwich. It's got some real meat in it."

She smirked at him, and Mason was tempted to stay in the back room a little longer, but work called. He'd been bringing his laptop since Thanksgiving, and that had made the writing go much faster. There was no doubt that the transition had been due to Livvy calling him out on his superstitions.

She knew most of the plot by now, except for the climax

and the ending. He didn't even know the exact ending. With Livvy bringing him lunch, he'd be able to continue writing at the library longer—which was where he was the most productive. In the cabin, he found himself pacing the floors, staring at the towering pines, or giving in and watching football.

He sat back down to write, and the next two hours flew by, which was always a good sign.

A text pulled him out of his focus. He checked his phone to see that Dawson had texted. They'd had a few conversations, had even met for lunch one day, but this invitation was unexpected. Dawson had invited him to watch the bowl game at his place. *The guys will all be coming.*

It didn't take much deduction to know that *the guys* included Slade.

Mason stared at the text for a few minutes. Dawson had told him that Slade knew about him and Livvy, and so Mason wasn't quite sure how hanging out in the same group would turn out. Would Slade be cool, friendly? Would they ignore each other? Would Slade say something stupid?

Mason exhaled. Although he was in Pine Valley for only a couple more weeks, he had nothing to hide. And Slade would just have to live with that.

Mason texted back: *I can come for a little while.* He wanted to also spend time with Livvy. Seeing her every day at the library was great and all, but he found that he liked spending evenings with her. No writing, no revising, just Livvy.

He returned to his laptop, figuring he could get in another hour of writing. His word count was nearing seventy-six thousand, and while most of his books were eighty to ninety thousand words, he usually ended up fleshing out some scenes while he was in the second draft stage.

Pilot was in the process of turning his life around,

although the demons were still hitting hard. His girlfriend, named Renee, was a lot like Livvy, Mason realized. Renee saw what needed to be done and did it. Even when it meant she put her own life at risk when she intercepted a drug deal.

"Hey, I'm off," Livvy's voice cut in.

Mason's thoughts reverted from story world to library world.

Livvy looped her arms about his neck from behind and rested her chin on his shoulder.

Mason powered down his laptop.

"No fair you won't let me read anything," she said, her warm breath tickling his neck.

"Soon," he said. "Only a few chapters to go." He turned his head toward her, catching her cinnamon scent. Maybe he wouldn't go to Dawson's.

"Hey," Livvy said. "I know you're planning on telling me your long, sad story tonight, but Felicity wants some help decorating the bookshop. And she can only do it after hours."

Mason nodded. "Sure, come over after that." They'd pretty much established hanging out at the cabin as their choice of location. Mason had no roommates, and well, it was a nice cabin. "Dawson invited me to his place to watch the bowl game."

"Oh, yeah?"

Mason didn't really like the excitement in her voice. She was always encouraging him to get to know more people in Pine Valley. A way of getting him to maybe move here . . . on one hand, he was flattered; on the other hand, he did have a life in San Diego.

"Okay then," Livvy said, her voice more perky. "You do your thing, I'll go do my thing, then we can hook up later." She released him and straightened, and Mason felt the loss of her touch immediately.

He watched her walk away, her bag slung over her shoulders, wearing no coat—of course—and no boots, despite the snow outside. Tonight they should really talk about when he was leaving. They had to be realistic.

Or maybe they could talk tomorrow, or the next day. Mason wasn't quite ready to pop their bubble.

He wrote for another hour. By the time he left the library, the bowl game had already started, but it wasn't like Mason had to be on time or anything. When he pulled up to Dawson's place, there were lots of cars in the parking lot. But Mason had no idea which car or truck belonged to who. He snatched the sack of food he'd picked up along the way, then climbed out of his Jeep.

Mason knocked on Dawson's apartment door, and moments later Dawson opened it with a grin. "You're late."

So apparently he could be late.

Mason handed Dawson the sack of food. "Brought some stuff."

"Thanks, man," Dawson said. "Come in and join the gang."

The living room of Dawson's apartment was crowded with about eight guys. Dawson pointed Mason to a kitchen chair that he'd brought in just as a touchdown was scored. Everyone jumped from their seats and cheered, except for a dark-haired man who groaned.

"Jeff's cheering for the other team," Dawson told Mason with a laugh.

Jeff looked over at Mason. "Who's your team?"

Mason glanced at the giant TV screen. "Neither." His gaze also caught the faces of the other men in the room. And yep. Slade was in the group. Slade didn't look away from the TV though. Who knew the doctor was such a football nut?

"That's great to hear," Jeff said, rising from his spot and extending a hand. "I'm Jeff Finch."

Mason refocused on Jeff, knowing that it would be seconds before Slade realized who'd joined the party.

"Jeff's a real estate agent," Dawson told Mason. "Watch out or he'll be selling you property before you know it."

Jeff's brows rose. "Are you looking? Single or family dwelling?"

Mason cleared his throat. "Uh, I'm renting a cabin for a bit while I finish my book."

"Oh . . . *you're* the writer," Jeff said, casting a significant look at Dawson.

Dawson only smirked and moved away.

"You're from San Diego, right?" Jeff continued.

"Yeah, that's me," Mason said, wondering why the room suddenly seemed very quiet. Had someone muted the game? He could practically feel Slade's gaze boring into him. Hadn't Dawson told his friends who else he'd invited?

"Cool," Jeff said. "I wish I had more time to read."

Mason nodded as if he understood. Some people considered reading a luxury, but then they spent hours every day watching TV or football or whatever their poison was.

Mason sat in one of the empty chairs, and Jeff took the seat next to him. Apparently they were now friends, and Mason wondered if Dawson had been completely serious warning him about being pitched on real estate by Jeff.

"I can't imagine even trying to write a book," Jeff said. "I mean, how do you keep all the characters and events straight?"

Mason shrugged. It was a common question from readers. "It's sort of like watching a movie or a television series. You get introduced to one set of characters and plotline at the same time. It's the same with writing. You create a character at a time, then figure out how that character interacts with others and the world around him."

Jeff actually looked interested. But the atmosphere of an intense football game with a bunch of guys probably wasn't the place to wax poetic. Some great play happened, and the men cheered again.

Jeff rubbed his face. "It looks like I'm doomed."

Mason focused on the game, purposefully not looking over at Slade.

Dawson settled into the chair on the other side of Mason. "I put all the food in the kitchen, so you can load up a plate whenever you want to."

"Thanks," Mason said.

Jeff turned to Mason again. "So how long are you in Pine Valley? And have you ever thought of having a second home?"

"I'm only here for a couple more weeks," Mason said. "The cabin owner has other renters coming in for Christmas." As soon as he said it, he regretted revealing that bit of information. Since he and Livvy hadn't discussed particulars, he'd hate for her to hear about it from someone else.

"It's about time," someone muttered.

At first Mason thought the comment had something to do with the football game, but by the way the room suddenly went silent, he realized that the comment had come from Slade.

Now Mason couldn't ignore the guy, as much as it would be the easy way out. He looked over to where Slade was perched on the edge of the couch. The man's green eyes were on Mason.

"Hey man, chill," Dawson said to Slade.

Slade only seemed to tense more.

Really? Was the idiot doctor going to suddenly decide that Livvy was worth more than the dirt he'd treated her as?

"I should go," Mason said under his breath.

"What's going on?" Jeff said, looking from Mason to Slade, then to Dawson.

"Nothing," Mason said and rose to his feet.

Across the room, Slade stood, his gaze not moving from Mason.

Dawson stood as well. "Don't leave, Mason. Things are cool. Football's the great equalizer, right?" He laughed and looked about the room, but no one laughed with him.

Now Jeff was on his feet. "Have I missed something?"

Jeff was tall and broad, and Mason hoped the guy would be on his side. But all these men had probably been best friends their entire lives, so the smart thing for Mason to do was leave.

Leave Dawson's place, and leave Pine Valley.

"He's dating Livvy," Slade said, his tone clipped. Cold. Clinical.

Heat pulsed through Mason, and he felt all eyes focus on him.

"Wow, I didn't realize," Jeff said, his voice a mixture of surprise and humor. "Awkward."

"Yeah," Slade continued. "I don't think we'll be too sad to see him go. Then Livvy will finally come to her senses."

Mason should just leave. Now. Let Slade have the final word. Instead, Mason stepped forward. "Livvy came to her senses on her own. You only have yourself to blame, *Doc*."

It was obvious that Slade wasn't expecting Mason's comeback. Slade blinked, his jaw tight, his shoulders stiff.

Mason took another step, and Dawson's hand clamped on his shoulder.

But Mason wasn't finished. "If you were ever off your phone for more than five minutes," he told Slade, "maybe you'd see the value of the people in your life who aren't *paying* you to spend time with them."

Just then Slade's phone rang, and Mason wanted to laugh at the irony. But he was still too pissed.

Slade's face reddened, and he pulled out the phone from his pocket, then read the screen. A panicked look crossed his face, and Mason finally did laugh.

"Go ahead and answer it," Mason ground out. "You know you're not the only doctor in town. And once you understand that you aren't God's gift, you'll appreciate the real relationships in your life."

Slade's phone stopped ringing, so now the only sound was the sports announcer on TV talking about an illegal helmet grab.

No one spoke. No one seemed to be moving. A muscle twitched in Slade's jaw.

Slade's phone rang again, and this time he did answer it. His face went red, but he spoke into the phone in a controlled, calm manner. Ever the professional doctor.

Slade strode past Mason and walked into the kitchen.

"Well, I think I'd better go," Mason told the room at large. "Sorry to bring the drama." He felt he'd gotten his point across, even if it meant all the men in this room now hated him. And if nothing else, he'd at least defended Livvy.

"That was awesome," Jeff said, his eyes flashing with mirth.

"Glad I could entertain," Mason said.

"Don't go," Dawson said. "Slade will probably be leaving any second by the sound of his conversation."

"Yeah, stay," one of the other men said. "I'm glad you told Slade why Livvy dumped him. He needs to get over himself."

"Sit," Dawson said, his hand on Mason's shoulder again. "Really. Slade needs to get used to you being around."

Mason met Dawson's gaze and noted the acceptance and challenge in it.

Mason decided to take the challenge. "Okay."

Dawson grinned.

Mason realized Dawson was right. Slade came out of the kitchen a couple of minutes later, mumbled a goodbye while managing not to make eye contact with Mason, then left.

A few moments later, Mason fixed himself a plate of food and found that he was quite hungry.

Twenty-two

*L*ivvy stood on a ladder, stretching to hang the garland along the top of the bookcase. Decorating the bookshop with Felicity had taken longer than she'd thought, and she was surprised Mason hadn't called her yet. Maybe that was a good sign though. Livvy selfishly wanted Mason to have friends in Pine Valley. Even though he seemed perfectly happy playing the reclusive writer type, Livvy felt the more connections he had around here, the better.

Because she was dreading him returning to San Diego. She wanted him to stay, but how could she ask him to? How could she expect him to? Of course there was always the other option . . . *she* could move to San Diego. But that would be more like a major commitment. And she couldn't let her heart even hope that Mason was in love with her and wanted to spend the rest of his life with her.

Livvy sighed despite the cheerful Christmas music playing from the Bluetooth speaker Felicity had next to the cash register.

"He hasn't called yet?" Felicity said, coming to stand by the ladder.

Livvy didn't need to check her phone to know it was turned on, and the volume was all the way up. "No."

"I thought you were happy he was hanging out with 'the guys.'" Felicity batted her lashes in exaggeration.

"I *am* happy."

Felicity laughed. "You could have fooled me." Tonight she wore a red sweater and red glasses. Although Felicity didn't need prescription glasses, she liked the fashion statement.

Livvy found it endearing.

"Are you going to ask him the big question tonight?" Felicity handed up another swag of garland.

The big question. About Christmas.

"Are you staying in town?" Livvy asked.

"I think I'll go to my parents for a day or two," Felicity said.

From what Livvy understood, things were pretty quiet in Felicity's household since she was an only child.

"I don't know how Mason will act if I invite him to my family's place for Christmas," Livvy said. "I mean, it would take things to another level. And I worry that it will turn off Mason if I even suggest it."

Felicity fell quiet for a moment. "Maybe ask him what his Christmas tradition is, then you can go from there."

"Good idea." Livvy blew out a breath and climbed down the ladder. "I'm still a ball of nerves."

Felicity grinned.

"What?"

"It's good to see you happy and not pining after some doctor fantasy."

Livvy grimaced. "Don't remind me. I saw Slade the other day at the grocery store. Thankfully I was with Mallory, and we only exchanged very brief hellos."

Felicity's brows shot up. "Any regrets? Any pining?"

"Nothing." Livvy picked up the ladder and moved it several feet down the aisle. "Which I guess is good to know. Even when . . . Mason leaves . . . there's no way Slade will ever be in the picture."

"I'm glad to hear that," Felicity said. "Because I think you have a visitor."

Livvy turned to see Mason opening the door of the bookshop. It was after hours, but the lights inside made it no secret that they were both decorating in here.

She found herself stupidly grinning as he walked in.

"Wow, looks great in here," he said.

His blue eyes met hers, then cut to Felicity. Then he looked at Livvy again and smiled. That heart-stopping smile, making Livvy's insides all gooey.

"I'm going to get that thing in the back," Felicity said.

Livvy barely heard her. She could only see Mason as he walked toward her. He stopped in front of her, and she breathed in his scent of clean, and musk, and the faint smell of leather that reminded her of his Jeep.

"Are you about done?" his voice was casual enough, but Livvy sensed an undercurrent there. He hadn't come to hang out in a bookstore.

Still, she had the urge to press her mouth against those lips of his. "Almost," she said.

"You're good to go," Felicity called out from someplace in the store. "I'm going to lock up soon and get home for some hot chocolate."

Mason's mouth quirked in question.

"She really likes hot chocolate," Livvy whispered.

"I heard that," Felicity said, laughter in her voice. But she was still keeping to the back room.

So Livvy stepped up to Mason and raised up on her toes to kiss the edge of his jaw.

Mason slipped his hand into hers, and instead of returning her kiss, he said, "Let's go."

"Okay," Livvy said, her nerves starting up. Mason had something on his mind, and she wasn't sure if that was good or bad. She reveled in the warmth and strength of his fingers enclosing hers. Surely he wouldn't be holding her hand if he had bad news to tell her, right?

Mason opened the bookshop door, and the cold air swirled around Livvy as they walked out together.

"Do I even need to ask if you brought a coat?" Mason said, his tone wry.

"I didn't want to drag it around," she said.

"Of course not." Mason slowed his step. "Did you drive?"

"No, I rode over with Felicity."

Mason nodded and led her to his Jeep, which was still running. He opened the door for her, and she climbed inside.

As he walked around the front of the Jeep, Livvy's heart thumped hard. What was going on? A dozen thoughts entered her mind, but she was too afraid to dwell on any of them.

"How was the game?" Livvy asked once he climbed in.

He glanced over at her. "Started out a little rough, then got better."

"Who was playing?"

Mason didn't answer for a moment, and it seemed his mind was someplace else.

Livvy tried to relax and took a couple of deep breaths. On one hand, she knew Mason liked her. On the other hand, he had a completely different life from her in another city hundreds of miles away.

"We need to talk about some things," Mason said.

Livvy's stomach knotted. There it was. The dreaded words. They were about to discuss their future, or the impossibility of it.

"Okay," she said, her voice sounding like a squeak.

Mason said nothing the rest of the drive to his cabin. Since Livvy didn't have her car, if there was some sort of argument between them, or even an official breakup, it would be really awkward getting home after. She could only imagine a totally silent car ride. Much like this one.

Finally they reached the cabin, and like the gentleman he always was, he parked, then came around to open her door. He didn't hold her hand as they walked in through the garage door that connected to the house.

He turned on a lamp in the great room, and the yellow glow should have cast a comforting light over everything, but it all seemed stark right now. Livvy shivered. The cabin was warm, but the vastness of it made her wish she had her coat on. She sat on the couch, unsure what else to do.

Mason didn't sit by her, but instead he crossed to the hearth and flipped on the gas fireplace. He stood there for a few moments, staring down at the flames.

Livvy couldn't stand the silence, or his brooding, or whatever this was, a moment longer.

"Are you mad at me?" she asked in a quiet voice.

He rubbed the back of his neck, still not looking at her. "No, I'm mad at myself."

Livvy felt her eyes burn—and she didn't even know what was going on. She just knew that something was terribly wrong. "Why?" she managed to say.

Mason finally turned to look at her. He folded his arms. "Slade was at Dawson's."

Livvy felt like the breath had been knocked out of her.

"We had words," he continued.

She couldn't keep sitting, so she moved to her feet. "What does that mean? Did you guys get into a fight or something?" She scanned his face for signs of bruising, but there was nothing.

"He called me out, and I called him out."

Livvy blinked. "What did you say?"

"Nothing that I haven't said before." Mason dropped his arms and slipped his hands into his pockets. "His phone rang like always, and he ended up leaving. I stayed to finish watching the game, and now Jeff Finch thinks I'm his best friend. He offered to look for a place for me to live."

Livvy didn't know if she'd heard him right . . . Did this mean . . .? She didn't dare hope, but it had blossomed anyway.

"I'm going back to San Diego on the twenty-third, whether my book is finished or not," Mason said. "The cabin owner has another family coming in for Christmas."

Livvy blinked. And then her eyes started to burn. Just like that . . . She'd *known* this would be the result from the very beginning. He'd never made it a secret that he'd leave after his book was done.

"That's like, in a week . . ." She stopped talking because it was impossible to mask the tremble in her voice.

Mason nodded. "I probably should have told you sooner. Jolene informed me a couple of weeks ago, but I was selfish, living in my own little world. Writing every day, spending my free time with you, ignoring the rest of life."

Livvy's throat went dry.

"Jolene is setting up a three-week book tour in January for me," he said. "It's been a few years since I've done one, and she thinks it will reconnect me to my readers. I'll be going to all the major cities in the nation. My new book will be on preorder, and we're depending on the preorder sales to make or break future book contracts."

"I think that's ... great," Livvy managed to say. "It sounds like a really smart marketing push."

Mason rubbed at his chin and looked away from her. It felt as if there were a million miles between them instead of a few steps. When he met her gaze again, there was an intensity in his eyes that made Livvy wish she'd stayed seated.

"Here's the thing, Livvy ... I'm in love with you." He exhaled, and all she could do was stare at him.

"We knew from the beginning that we were on different tracts in life," he continued, "and I didn't mean for things to get complicated. And I especially don't want to hurt you. But the reality is that once this book tour is done, I'll be writing the next book. Then the launch will come for my new book. The cycle is vicious, and I can't keep hiding out here in Pine Valley, avoiding what I've been avoiding."

Livvy wiped at the tears that had fallen onto her cheeks.

"I have a little more than a week left here," he said. "I'm going to write the final chapters, read through the whole manuscript, then send it to Jolene. By then it will be time to return to San Diego and prepare for my book tour. It's not fair to ask you to follow me around the country or to relocate to San Diego. Despite my feelings for you, I am new to all of this. I can't guarantee anything, so it's better to not make any promises in the first place."

Livvy stepped back and sank onto the couch. She hated that she was crying, but she hated more that Mason's honesty was breaking her heart. He was right ... of course he was right. It wasn't like he was going to propose marriage and sell his house, or ask her to find a librarian job in San Diego. No, they both had their own careers, their own lives. Their paths had just intersected at a strange time in Mason's life.

She took a deep, steadying breath and looked up at Mason. His gaze was still on her. "I'm not asking for any promises, Mason," she said, "if that's what you're worried about. And I know the risks as much as you do." She rubbed her hands over her knees, trying to warm up the cold trembling. "I'm still trying to get used to the idea that I've fallen in love with a man who's not a doctor."

Mason reached her in three strides and tugged her to her feet. He crushed her against him, and she clung to him, feeling his heart beating as fast as hers.

"We're both fools, then," he whispered.

She laughed, although the tears had started again. He pressed his lips against her neck. She closed her eyes and let her senses become lost in the smell of him, the soft fabric of his shirt against her cheek, his warm arms encircling her.

She knew that if he asked, right now, for her to leave Pine Valley with him, she'd say yes. But that wasn't what he was asking. She'd both seen and heard the hesitation, the uncertainty in his voice, the questions he had . . . She didn't want him to ever regret his decisions. So she would wait. As long as it took.

"Livvy," Mason murmured against her ear. "I'm going to miss you."

Twenty-three

Three Months Later

Livvy opened her mailbox, grateful that the snow was finally starting to melt. It had been a long winter—especially after Mason had left Pine Valley. She pulled out the padded envelope from the mailbox. Her eyes widened at the sight of Mason's return address scrawled in the left corner of the envelope. By the weight of the package, she guessed it was his new book.

It wouldn't come out until June, but he had said he'd send her an ARC—which she'd learned was an Advanced Reader's Copy. ARCs went out to reviewers, journalists, bloggers, and select marketing contacts.

Livvy nearly skipped to the front door of her house. Thankfully Mallory was working the evening shift at the library, so Livvy had the house to herself. She set the package on the kitchen table, where the light from the late afternoon sun turned the tan envelope into a rectangle of gold.

She shed her jacket, then sat down and picked up the package. First she gazed at the handwriting. A small thrill ran through her as she thought of Mason penning her name, then writing out her address. She looked at the return address again. She'd sent a Christmas card to his San Diego address after he left Pine Valley. Then she'd sent a New Year's card and a Valentine's card.

Mason had thanked her for all of them, then had informed her that he wasn't a card writer.

"That's probably because you use up all your words in your books," she told him.

Since Mason's departure, Livvy had run into Slade a handful of times. She'd said hi but hadn't left any room for conversation. He'd called on Christmas Day, which she'd ignored, and then again about two weeks later. She'd ignored that call, too.

With or without Mason in Pine Valley, Livvy had no desire to return to her former fantasy of becoming a doctor's wife. She and Mason had talked on the phone almost every night. Sometimes for a few minutes, sometimes for hours. He'd tell her about his grueling schedule, and she'd tell him her library adventures. He'd finally told her why he didn't like turkey, and Livvy had never heard a more heartbreaking story. Once in a while he'd tell her about his current plot—those were the conversations she loved the most because she felt honored that he trusted her in such a way.

And always, at the end of every conversation, he'd say he missed her.

Livvy always held back her tears until she'd hung up the phone with him.

Now she turned the padded envelope over and opened the sealed flap. Mason had told her that the final cover wasn't usually on the ARCs, so when she pulled out the book, she wasn't surprised to see that the cover was a plain blue, with simply the title and author name.

Bruise

Mason Rowe

A well of warmth filled her chest. He'd done it. He'd finished his book. He'd broken through his block.

Livvy had no doubt she'd be up all night reading about Pilot. She opened the cover, careful not to open it too far since she didn't want to crease any pages.

The title page was much the same. Then she turned to the next page.

The words in the middle of the page stopped her. She didn't recall him putting in dedication pages before. But he'd added one this time.

For my favorite librarian.

Livvy laughed. Then she hugged the book against her chest and closed her eyes. She'd never felt so much joy and anguish in the same moment. Joy because she was so happy for Mason, and anguish because he was so far away. After a few moments, she wiped her tears, then she went and changed into comfy clothing to prepare for her reading binge. She fixed a bowl of trail mix and grabbed a water bottle, then continued into the living room, curled up on the couch, and began to read.

She wouldn't be able to call and thank him until later tonight because he had some sort of library event, he'd said. Which was ironic because his agent had never approved him doing one at the Pine Valley Library.

Well, it couldn't be helped.

She began to read.

Although Pilot was being put through the wringer, Livvy smiled as she read, remembering the plot points that Mason had discussed with her. It was as if he were whispering in her ear as she read. She could hear his voice, his turn of phrase, his likes and dislikes, his moods, his passions throughout the scenes.

Livvy hadn't realized how much time had passed until she was forced to turn on lights. She moved about the living room, switching on lamps just as Mallory walked in the door.

"Hey, there's some mail for you," Mallory said.

"What?" Livvy frowned. "I already got the mail."

Mallory handed over a business-sized envelope, and Livvy's breath caught when she recognized the handwriting. Mallory continued into the kitchen and started rummaging through the fridge.

Livvy didn't move for a moment. The envelope had no stamp on it, yet it was from Mason. She closed her eyes, realizing that the padded envelope with the book hadn't had any stamps on it either. Had . . . Mason come to Pine Valley?

She ripped open the envelope and withdrew a folded piece of paper. There were three lines written on it.

My new address:
582 Cedar Road
Pine Valley

Livvy let out a yelp.

"Are you okay?" Mallory came out of the kitchen.

"I—I've got to go."

"What's going on?" Mallory asked.

"I'm not sure, but I think everything is going to be fine." She hugged a confused Mallory, then grabbed her keys from the hook by the door. Livvy hurried outside and jumped into her car, then she drove toward the Pine Valley ski resort, where the familiar address was located.

She tried her best to drive at a reasonable speed, and she

forced herself to take steady, deep breaths so she wouldn't hyperventilate. When she pulled up at the cabin that Mason had rented in the winter, she could hardly believe she was here again.

This had better not be some horrible joke.

She jumped out of the car and took deliberate steps along the walkway leading to the front door, when in fact she wanted to run.

She hadn't been here since Mason had left; she couldn't bear to drive by the place. Nothing looked disturbed and no lights shone from the windows. She took a deep breath and rang the doorbell instead of pounding on it like a crazed woman.

The chimes sounded from within, so stately and melodic.

Then the door opened.

And he was standing there.

Just like he had so many times before. His hair was shorter, his jaw clean-shaven, and he wasn't wearing layers. His pale blue button-down shirt matched his eyes.

"How long have you been here?" she whispered.

"Three hours and twenty minutes," he said in that low voice of his that was *so* much better in person. His eyes made a slow perusal of her, and she realized she was wearing her oldest yoga pants, with bleach stains, and a T-shirt with at least three holes in it. His mouth quirked. "I thought you'd never come."

Livvy stepped through the doorway and into his arms. He drew her against him and buried his face into her hair. Livvy had so many questions, and her stomach was fluttering like mad, but all she could think of was that Mason was *back*. She didn't know why or for how long, but right now she didn't care.

"I got the book, but I guess I missed the letter," Livvy said, drawing away, still not believing Mason was here in the flesh. She ran her hands over his shoulders just to be sure. "Mallory brought it in after work. And I guess I missed the fact that there was no postage on the package either."

Mason's blue eyes were intent on hers as he lifted his hand and ran his thumb along her jaw, then down her neck. His touch was like a trail of fire along her skin.

"I read the dedication," Livvy said, her voice catching. "I never imagined that you'd dedicate the book to me."

The edges of Mason's lips curved just before he leaned down and kissed her oh-so-gently. "I think it was a given." He reached past her and shut the open door, then he cradled her face with both hands. "I missed you like crazy."

Then he was kissing her for real, and as his mouth explored hers, she thought she'd combust into a thousand tiny pins of light. He was real. More than real.

She skimmed her fingers up his chest, then along his neck at his open collar. His skin was warm and smooth, and his pulse was beating as fast as hers. "So . . ." Livvy breathed, when Mason allowed her to. "Are you renting this for another writing stint?"

Mason tucked her hair behind her ear, then let his hands linger on her shoulders. "I bought it."

Livvy blinked. "What? How? I mean . . . I thought—"

He pressed a finger against her lips and scanned her face. "My beach house in San Diego sold for about twice what I expected." He lowered his hands and grasped hers. "I had planned to get one of the condos that Jeff Finch had sent pictures of, but then I kept thinking about this cabin. And all the memories. And how it kind of felt like my cabin already, or *our* cabin. Jeff called the owner and made an offer, and we closed on it yesterday."

Livvy couldn't move, couldn't speak.

"So unless you object, I'm here to stay in Pine Valley."

She laughed. "I . . . I can't believe it."

Mason grinned. "Good, because I'm buying you something with all-wheel-drive, too. I don't like you driving that little car up the canyon in the winter. Maybe a CRV or a 4Runner."

Livvy's mind couldn't keep up. "You can't buy me something like that. I mean, that would be a serious-girlfriend gift."

Mason released her hands and set his hands on her waist. "I was thinking of it as more of a *wife* gift."

"Mason," she whispered, her eyes filling with tears. "What are you saying?"

He kissed her forehead, and his clean scent seemed to encompass all the space around her.

"I've had a lot of time to think about everything," he said. "About you. About us. There's nothing I want more in this world than to share everything I have with you. You already have my heart."

Livvy blinked back her tears. "Well, if you're asking me to marry you, then I kind of wish I would have at least gotten dressed for the occasion."

Mason chuckled. "I don't mind." His gaze scanned her attire, and his mouth quirked, then he pressed a kiss just below her jaw, lingering. When he lifted his head, he whispered. "Marry me, Livvy Harmon. Be my happily ever after."

She stared into his blue eyes and saw the man she had missed so deeply and loved so completely. She'd known her answer for months. "Yes, Mason Rowe. I will marry you."

As Mason drew her into a long, slow kiss, Livvy knew that she wouldn't change the rocky path that had brought them together. Because this ending was the best Happily Ever After she could have ever dreamed up.

More Pine Valley Novels!

Heather B. Moore is a four-time *USA Today* bestselling author. She writes historical thrillers under the pen name H.B. Moore; her latest thrillers include *The Killing Curse* and *Breaking Jess*. Under the name Heather B. Moore, she writes romance and women's fiction. Her newest releases include the historical romances *Love is Come* and *Ruth*. She's also one of the coauthors of the *USA Today* bestselling series: A Timeless Romance Anthology. Heather writes speculative fiction under the pen name Jane Redd; releases include the Solstice series and *Mistress Grim*. Heather is represented by Dystel, Goderich & Bourret.

For book updates, sign up for Heather's email list: hbmoore.com/contact

Website: HBMoore.com

Facebook: Fans of H. B. Moore

Blog: MyWritersLair.blogspot.com

Instagram: @authorhbmoore

Twitter: @HeatherBMoore

Made in the USA
Coppell, TX
20 March 2022

75272525R00125